# A CANDLELIGHT ROMANCE

## CANDLELIGHT ROMANCES

214 Pandora's Box, BETTY HALE HYATT
215 Safe Harbor, JENNIFER BLAIR
216 A Gift of Violets, JANETTE RADCLIFFE
217 Stranger on the Beach, ARLENE HALE
218 To Last a Lifetime, JENNIFER BLAIR
219 The Way to the Heart, GAIL EVERETT
220 Nurse in Residence, ARLENE HALE
221 The Raven Sisters, DOROTHY MACK
222 When Dreams Come True, ARLENE HALE
223 When Summer Ends, GAIL EVERETT
224 Love's Surprise, GAIL EVERETT
225 The Substitute Bride, DOROTHY MACK
226 The Hungry Heart, ARLENE HALE
227 A Heart Too Proud, LAURA LONDON
228 Love Is the Answer, LOUISE BERGSTROM
229 Love's Untold Secret, BETTY HALE HYATT
230 Tender Longings, BARBARA LYNN
231 Hold Me Forever, MELISSA BLAKELY
232 The Captive Bride, LUCY PHILLIPS STEWART
233 Unexpected Holiday, LIBBY MANSFIELD
234 One Love Forever, MEREDITH BABEAUX BRUCKER
235 Forbidden Yearnings, CANDICE ARKHAM
236 Precious Moments, SUZANNE ROBERTS
237 Surrender to Love, HELEN NUELLE
238 The Heart Has Reasons, STEPHANIE KINCAID
239 The Dancing Doll, JANET LOUISE ROBERTS
240 My Lady Mischief, JANET LOUISE ROBERTS
241 The Heart's Horizons, ANNE SHORE
242 A Lifetime to Love, ANN DABNEY
243 Whispers of the Heart, ANNE SHORE
244 Love's Own Dream, JACQUELINE HACSI
245 La Casa Dorada, JANET LOUISE ROBERTS
246 The Golden Thistle, JANET LOUISE ROBERTS
247 The First Waltz, JANET LOUISE ROBERTS
248 The Cardross Luck, JANET LOUISE ROBERTS
249 The Searching Heart, SUZANNE ROBERTS
250 The Lady Rothschild, SAMANTHA LESTER
251 Bride of Chance, LUCY PHILLIPS STEWART
252 A Tropical Affair, ELISABETH BERESFORD
253 The Impossible Ward, DOROTHY MACK
254 Victim of Love, LEE CANADAY
255 The Bad Baron's Daughter, LAURA LONDON
256 Winter Kisses, Summer Love, ANNE SHORE

# Close to the Stars

Meredith Babeaux Brucker

A CANDLELIGHT ROMANCE

Published by
Dell Publishing Co, Inc.
1 Dag Hammarskjold Plaza
New York, New York 10017

Copyright © 1978 by Meredith Babeaux Brucker

All rights reserved. No part of this
book may be reproduced or transmitted in any form or by
any means, electronic or mechanical, including photo-
copying, recording or by any information storage
and retrieval system, without the written permission
of the Publisher, except where permitted by law.

Dell ® TM 681510, Dell Publishing Co., Inc.

ISBN: 0-440-11021-1

Printed in the United States of America

First printing—April 1979

*Close to the Stars*

# CHAPTER ONE

The mist had crept through the valley at dawn, touching every blade of grass in the field and leaving a beading of moisture that now glistened in the morning sun. Bonita watched her own steps with the idle interest of someone with nothing better to do. She noticed that the soles of her boots flattened the grass momentarily with each step, but when she looked behind her she could see that the meadow fescue sprang back up again just as if she had never been there. She wondered if her whole life would be like that. Would she ever make a permanent mark upon the world, or was she destined to spend all her days in the quiet isolation of Carmel Valley ranch life, leaving no impression on the grassy fields she walked through?

She strolled farther from the ranch house, toward the lower end of the field that fronted on the main highway through the valley. She remembered when horses used to graze here and how they would gather in a group along the front fence in the afternoon as if interested in watching the passing parade of cars heading toward the ocean and the seaside community of Carmel, or inland through the pass in the hills and then northward to Salinas or, eventually, San Francisco.

Her grandmother no longer kept horses, and the barns and corrals as well as this pastureland stood empty, a mocking emphasis of Bonita's loneliness. The only animal left on the place was Lark, and at the thought of her dog she looked around for him, suddenly noticing that he was not sniffing the ground close behind her heels as he usually did during her morning walks.

She hugged her rough wool plaid shirt closer to her body for warmth, for the morning sunlight had still not warmed the day. As she walked on, she let her mind roam freely, thinking about the story she was writing and the notebook back on her desk with the first scribblings of that new idea. She had filled several notebooks in the last few years, as she had filled her life with the stories of people and places in this valley. But now she felt a new urgency about putting her words on paper. She was no longer a schoolgirl weaving fantasies. She was beginning to see herself as a writer with something to say that could entertain and enchant those who read her words.

The change in her attitude had come quite recently when her grandmother had convinced her to type up one of her stories and send it to a national magazine. At first Bonita had been reluctant, for she was afraid the story would be turned down and she wasn't sure she could take such rejection. But Alberta Langmeade had a determined nature, and she had nagged Bonita so much that Bonita finally submitted the story. When an acceptance letter came from the editor, Bonita was overjoyed, and Alberta was as proud as if it were her own work. It almost was, for it was the love story of Bonita's father and mother, and Bonita had learned it from her grandmother during long evenings by the fire.

After the story was published in the magazine, the editor wrote to Bonita again saying the story had received exceptional response from his readers. In fact, he informed her, her story had even been noticed by people at a movie studio in Hollywood.

Then came the letter from Magnet Studios. It was typed on paper that felt so stiff in her hands that it might have been a parchment scroll containing a decree from an emperor of an ancient kingdom. Actually it was from a Mr. Jordan McCaslin, offering her a royal sum of money for the movie rights to her story. When she accepted his offer, he sent her another letter offering her the job of writing the first draft of the movie script.

Bonita had been thrilled at the opportunity, and she'd thrown all her energies into the project. For the past three months she had worked on the script night and day, finally sending it off to the studio when she was sure it was just right. Now, with such positive response to her writing, she was motivated to work even harder on new material. She was spinning out story possibilities all the time. In the morning stillness of her walks the seeds germinated in her mind.

*That story about the man who keeps bees would work better if I put his sister into it. She's such a good character. I wonder if it would make a good movie. Maybe I could build up the part about their house burning down. That would make an exciting scene.*

She pulled out a stubby pencil and a piece of paper and made a note. Then she stuffed them back into the pocket of her jeans.

She knew it was risky to dream too much about a future as a scriptwriter, but as she continued walking she let herself picture the people she knew, the places she loved, in scenes played out in cinematic color, blown up into screen-size images, being enjoyed by audiences in movie theaters all across the country.

The large pasture Bonita loved to explore was bisected by a dirt road that led from the main highway up to her grandmother's house. Bonita's steps had brought her to the white rail fence that bordered the road, and she bent over, her small body sliding easily through the fence rails. As she straightened up she was startled to hear a whimpering sound, and glanced over to see her golden retriever lying in the middle of the roadway, his big ochre body uncharacteristically immobile.

"Oh, Lark. What's wrong?" she called out as she ran toward him.

Lark lifted his head as she knelt beside him, and the ochre plume of his tail moved slowly back and forth flat on the ground, clearing a smooth place in the sandy soil. His eyes showed a mixture of pain and exasperation, for he liked nothing better than a romp with Bonita, and this morning he was missing that opportunity.

Bonita ran her small fingers quickly over the dog, examining him for broken bones or any swellings or bruises. She was sure Lark hadn't been hit by a car, for this road was used very little. Visitors to the ranch were rare.

"You naughty dog," Bonita exclaimed, with a relieved lilt to her voice that she knew the dog would understand better than the words themselves. "You've been out behind the barn exploring in those brambles again. Your paws are full of burrs. Now hold still."

Bonita went to work quickly, holding the soft pads of Lark's paws in her hand and trying to extract the prickly weed pods as gently as possible.

"Oh, darn. I can't see what I'm doing," she said as she brushed a strand of her dark hair out of her face. She stood up and removed the hat she'd been wearing. It was a funny old tweed cap that had hung on a hook by the back door as long as she could remember. She guessed that it might have belonged to her father, but she had never asked her grandmother. She just grabbed it and wore it whenever the mornings were cold. Now it would come in handy, for it was large enough that all her hair could be easily stuffed up inside it, away from her face.

Her hair was soft and silky, and it kept slipping out

of her grasp. She finally forced every bit of it up into the cap, and then pulled down on the rough tweed to hold the hat firmly on her head and keep her hair out of the way. Lark's eyes beseeched her to hurry back to her work.

Bonita was concentrating so hard on what she was doing that she paid no attention to the sound of a car engine slowing down on the highway a few hundred feet away, nor did she particularly notice the change in sound as the wheels left the paving and thubbed along the dirt road toward her. Then all at once she was aware of the car, for she could hear the roar of an engine behind her, and the sound was getting unmistakably louder with each second. She dropped Lark's paw and placed her hand on the big dog's head for reassurance, then turned to look over her shoulder.

She realized that she was crouched down with the dog on a portion of the road that dipped slightly. If she didn't stand up and warn him, the driver of the car would not see them until he was almost on top of them, as he was driving at a speed that indicated he had little respect for private country roads. She jumped to her feet and began waving her arms in the air, confident that the red in her plaid shirt would attract his attention quickly and he would stop.

To her immense shock the car kept coming. Did he think he could merely swerve around her on this narrow driveway between the two long fences, or did he assume she would have to step aside for him? Seeming to answer her, the unseen driver of the large green sedan began honking his horn imperiously, commanding her to move.

There was probably a complicated formula to compute how fast the car was coming, how heavy the dog, and how much time was required for Bonita to lift the dog. But Bonita made all her calculations with one frightened sweep of her brown eyes from car to dog. It was clear to her that there was no time left in which to get the dog to safety. She had to make the car stop its unrelenting approach.

She waved again, but the rude bleat of the automobile horn was repeated in response, as if the stubborn driver was shouting his intention to keep going, to blast this annoying interference out of the way.

Bonita stamped one boot on the ground, frustrated by this battle of wills she was suddenly engaged in. Whoever was behind the wheel was not interested in what her problem might be, but only in getting where he was going without delay.

As the car came over the dip in the road, Bonita knew that the driver could at last see that there was a dog lying at her feet. She could hear the agonized sound of brakes sharply applied peal through the air. The car went into a twisting lurch as the driver tried to keep control of the vehicle and still make sure he didn't run right into the obstacle he was trying to avoid.

With the resisting sound of tires scraping sideways across sandy soil, the car careened just inches from Bonita and Lark, sending a spray of dirt over them as it passed. Then a terrible sound of splintered wood told Bonita the car had run into the fence, and she rubbed at the dirt in her eyes to see if it had finally come to a stop.

Bonita realized that if her willful adversary had refused to give in for just a second longer, he might have been unable to control the slide of the car, and she or Lark might have been injured. With relief Bonita threw herself down on Lark, hugging the dog and letting the fear she had held inside of her until now come out in a burst of tears.

"You stupid boy! Why didn't you get out of my way? Are you trying to get yourself killed out here in the middle of the street?"

Bonita couldn't believe the harsh words of attack when she had expected apologies and condolence. The voice had a grating sound to it, the words bitten off with unkind rage. She buried her face in the lovely softness of Lark's neck, almost hiding her face with his long ears as she held onto them for courage. She was so glad to feel Lark safe in her arms that she was reluctant to face the caustic arrogance of this enemy who had almost vanquished them.

He spoke again. "I think I deserve an explanation. The fence is busted, the car's probably scratched up. Now stand up and face me like a man and quit sniveling!"

Bonita felt a surge of indignation as she raised her head to look up at the stranger. The tears in her eyes clouded her vision and she hastily wiped them aside, wincing as the gritty sand on her cheeks turned to smears of mud. She sprang to her feet, but was surprised to realize that once she was standing the stranger still loomed over her.

He might have been a handsome young man, but at the moment his craggy face seemed gloomy and forbidding in its anger as he stared down at her. She raised herself onto her toes, stretching as tall as possible, but was unable to meet his gaze directly. So she stuffed her hands in her pockets and stared at the ground as she spat out her defense.

"My dog is hurt. I couldn't move him. And besides, this isn't a street, it's a private driveway, and you have no business being here."

At that moment a huge puffy cloud blown by high winds in the sky above them moved in front of the sun and the day darkened. Bonita looked up and noticed that the sky-blue eyes of the stranger dimmed at the same time, no longer catching the glints of sunlight. His sun-bleached hair suddenly darkened to brown as the highlighting beam of sunshine was extinguished. She shivered in the sudden coolness, and then she searched for a way to disturb his calm composure.

"You get off my property! You almost scared my dog to death," she said. They both looked down at Lark to verify her words.

Lark was panting, with the red-black interior of his mouth exposed so that it resembled a quarter-moon smile. He wagged his tail in response to their attention, cheerfully unaware that he had been in any danger. Bonita gave her dog a defeated frown, wishing he were a better actor.

The man turned his attention back to Bonita. She could see the scorn in his eyes as his impatience with her sketched the lines of a grimace across the classic perfection of his facial features.

"You're a feisty little guy, aren't you?" he said to her, as if he were flicking an irksome ant off a piece of pie at a picnic.

Bonita waited for him to ask what was wrong with her dog and offer his help and forgiveness, but he gave her a last dismissing look and then turned suddenly to head back toward the car.

He backed away from the broken fence, leaving a pile of wreckage that infuriated Bonita further.

"Are you going to pay for that fence?" she called, but her words were drowned out as the car wheels ground forward on the sand.

He was ignoring her warnings to leave the property, and heading right down the road in the direction he'd been going. She clenched her fists with angry impotence because the argument was unfinished. Then she realized that since the well-dressed young man was obviously on the wrong road, once he reached her grandmother's house he would discover his mistake and he would have to come back this way to leave. She smiled to herself, planning her insults and anticipating the victory of her next encounter with him.

She finished her work on Lark's paws and was happy to see the dog spring to his feet. He took a few careful steps, as if to check Bonita's work, and then gave an exuberant bounce in her direction and licked at her hand by way of thanks. As she started up the road toward the house, he fell in step behind her with a special verve to his gait.

It took her several minutes to reach the top of the driveway, where it branched into a wide circle in front of the big white farmhouse. A grove of tall buckeye trees planted in the center of the circle obscured her vision for a moment for they were always the first native trees to blossom every spring and they already had a thick sprinkling of green on their gaunt branches. Then she saw the car parked in front of the porch steps.

The rude stranger was nowhere in sight and she assumed he must have gone inside. She wondered why her grandmother hadn't already sent him on his way. Bonita went to the side of the house, through the vegetable garden to the back door. Lark tried as usual to follow her inside and she banged the door noisily to remind the persistent dog that her grandmother wanted him to remain outside.

"Bonita, is that you?" Alberta Langmeade called from the front room.

"Yes, Grandma."

"Come in here, dear, right away." There was a note of insistence to her grandmother's voice that made Bonita fear she might be having some trouble getting rid of the intruder, so Bonita hurried through the big old rooms of the house toward the sound of voices.

She was surprised to find her grandmother sitting quite calmly in her high-back wing chair beside the fireplace, with the stranger unfolded casually all over the couch opposite her, comfortable in his white turtleneck sweater, his blazer jacket slung over the back of a nearby chair. The firelight was reflecting off the changeable hue of his hair, making him appear as blond and tan-skinned as an athlete. As she entered the room he looked up to meet her questioning expression with a triumphant smile that indicated he felt completely welcome in her home.

"Oh, Bonita, you look a mess. No wonder Mr. McCaslin mistook you for a boy. Now come in and be introduced properly."

Bonita was too stunned to speak. So this was Jordan McCaslin, the man she only knew through official letters and contracts that came in the mail from his office at Magnet Studios. What a shock to discover him to be a man so lacking in compassion that he didn't even want to stop his car when there was a person in trouble in his way. Her lovely story, which she had dreamed of seeing made into a movie, couldn't possibly be put into the hands of this dreadfully selfish and unfeeling man!

She wondered what he was doing in Carmel. Did this mean there was something wrong with the script she had sent him? He was standing up to meet her, and again she felt as inconsequential as a naughty boy under his haughty stare.

"Mr. McCaslin, this is my granddaughter, Bonita Langmeade, the writer."

Bonita squirmed with embarrassment at her grandmother's proud label. Then seeing that he was reaching for a handshake she wiped her dirty hand quickly up and down the side of her jeans and offered it to him. His large tanned hand covered her small one completely, and his grip was strong enough to be both businesslike and masterful.

"Bonita, this is Jordan McCaslin. He's come all the way from Hollywood to talk to you. He's going to be personally producing your movie."

"My movie?" she asked.

Jordan McCaslin was quick but polite with his interjection. "Well, *my* movie, actually, if you'll excuse the correction, Mrs. Langmeade. We're going into production as soon as possible."

Bonita's grandmother apparently mistook her inability to speak for feelings of awe and was quick to try to rescue her.

"Now go and clean up a bit. Mr. McCaslin has been very patiently explaining to me what his job as head of production at the studio involves, and he's telling me what these movie people have to do before they start making a movie. I'll just let him go on and tell me more while we wait for you."

Bonita ran upstairs, pulling the cap off her head and feeling her soft hair tumble onto her shoulders. There was no time to make herself look decent, but at least she could try to clean off some of the grime this careless stranger had dirtied her with because of his haste to get where he was going.

She scrubbed her face, then watched in the bathroom mirror as her cheeks sprang to bright pink life under her rough towel. She applied some of her brightest new lipstick and ran a comb through her black hair to smooth out the tangles left by the cap.

As she turned to and fro in front of the mirror studying her small-boned but very womanly frame, she wondered peevishly how he could have mistaken her for a boy. He had certainly given her body a careful scrutiny while her grandmother was introducing them just now, and she realized with embarrassment that he was wondering, too, how he could have made the mistake. She removed the plaid shirt, and picked out a more form-fitting yellow and white checked blouse with a delicate lace trim on the collar and cuffs, hoping as she tucked it tightly into her jeans that it would give her as shapely and feminine a look as possible. She stuffed the legs of her jeans into the tops of her knee-high boots and, with a helpless sigh, headed downstairs, wishing there was time to do more to herself.

"Mr. McCaslin has just been telling me about some of the big box-office features he's produced," Mrs. Langmeade told Bonita as soon as she entered the room. Bonita couldn't help but smile affectionately at her grandmother, noticing how enthusiastically she was picking up the moviemaker's vocabulary.

"Did you know he produced *The Violent Victor* and *Death by War* and even *Murder on Monday*, wasn't it, Jordan? That was wonderful. Lots of suspense."

"Yes," he smiled smugly at her grandmother's praise.

Bonita shuddered at the specter of death and violence his titles evoked. She wondered what had ever attracted him to purchase her love story.

"I'll just go make us some tea while you two talk," her grandmother said. "I think there are some blueberry muffins left from breakfast, too. Will you excuse me?"

Jordan McCaslin walked immediately to Alberta's big chair by the fire and made himself at home in it. Bonita hung back, unsure of how to proceed in conversation now that she was left alone with him. Noticing her hesitation he smiled at her with a look of superiority that made it clear he was enjoying her discomfort, and then gestured for her to sit down across from him.

"Take a seat, my son." He obviously wasn't going to let her forget his first impression of her.

Bonita sat down and tried to cross her legs daintily, but the heavy walking boots spoiled the effect she was trying to achieve.

He watched her with amusement. "I'm sorry, but I just can't believe that you're Bonita Langmeade, the writer," he said with a teasing tang to his voice that she resented.

"Well, what did you expect?" she snapped.

"Oh, I don't know. I guess I pictured the writer of the love story as an older, more worldly woman. Certainly not a young tomboy."

"Can we just forget about this morning?" she said. "As soon as you pay for the fence, that is."

"I've already discussed that with your grandmother. I'll take care of it."

"Oh, I know you will. Money's no object, I'm sure. Incidentally, my dog is okay now. He just had some burrs in his feet. I'm sure you're concerned, even if you did forget to inquire."

"I could tell there was nothing seriously wrong with him. And look, I didn't come here to throw my money around. You're the one who seems to be intent upon getting the fence paid for. Rest assured it will be and let's get down to business."

"What business is that? You bought my story, you own it. I sent you the script you asked for. What more do you want?"

Jordan McCaslin stood up, tensely pushing his hand through his glinting brown hair. "Your hostile attitude is not making this easy, you know. I want your cooperation. Moviemaking is a team effort, and if any member of the team is unhappy, it can spread throughout the company."

"I will try to forget about your car almost running me down if you'll forget your mistake."

"I am well aware by now that you are a female if that's what is worrying you." He gave her a sideways look that she was sure he had perfected during his years of working with experienced actors. It was a look calculated to hint at flirtation and seduction, but the deep pool coolness in his eyes belied his pretense of romancing her.

She cleared her throat nervously. "Now, down to business as you suggested."

"I'm here to do some location scouting. I want to make this film in the Carmel area. The story takes place in the Carmel Valley and I think it has to be shot here because the location is almost one character in the story, as I see it."

Bonita nodded her agreement, but he seemed uninterested in whether she agreed with him or not.

"I would like to hear your suggestions, because you know the area well and we'll need to find the right location for every scene in the script," he said.

When Jordan McCaslin turned to work, he seemed transformed by his enthusiasm. Bonita could almost see the nervous energy of creativity course through his body as he gestured broadly discussing his newest project.

"You're not going to do any of the filming in Hollywood?" she asked.

"There aren't many interiors. So much of the action takes place outdoors that I think we can do it all here."

Bonita was disappointed. She had pictured herself going to Hollywood to watch the filming, having an exciting opportunity to leave the valley and sample a new and exotic place.

"Well, I'll show you the actual spots where the story took place," she said.

His attention had been internalized on the plans he was weaving, but suddenly he turned to look at her with an intensely concentrated look that unnerved her. She noticed that his eyes were like open sky, they were so blue, and tended to give off storm warnings when his emotions suddenly changed.

"But your story takes place just after the turn of the century," he said. "How do you know where the real story took place?" He was watching for her answer more intently than she felt it deserved.

"Oh, I've fudged a bit on the time period," she said. "I have to make some attempt to disguise the real people in my stories."

"Real people," he mused. Still distracted, he seemed to have to force his attention back to the film.

Bonita knew he was used to working with professional writers, and he probably felt that her approach to her work was sadly amateurish, basing her stories on people she knew. He would certainly laugh at her lack of imagination if he knew her love story was that of her own mother and father and how they had met and fallen in love while living on neighboring ranches here in the valley.

"I also want to talk to you about the script while I'm here. The first draft you sent me was a good start."

"You mean there's more to do?"

"There certainly is. In the movie business we always do a rough first draft and then a final version that is our shooting script. I would like you to write that final draft for me, if you're willing."

"What do you mean? I tried to make it as cinematic as I could."

"Yes, and you did a surprisingly good job for a newcomer to this business. But I have some suggestions for the rewrite. The story is just too delicate, too dreamlike the way it is now. We'll need to punch it up with some more action scenes. You know, give it more conflict. And our male lead needs to be a lot stronger."

Bonita was glad for an interruption while she absorbed these overbearing criticisms. Alberta Langmeade at that moment came into the room, her strong shoulders easily supporting the heavy tea tray. She placed it on the coffee table between them and then hurried out for some forgotten item, apparently oblivious to Bonita's stony silence as she called over her shoulder, "Pour the tea, dear."

Bonita made no move to offer her guest tea so he helped himself while saying to her, "Your story was not carved on stone tablets, you know. It is a living, changing thing that we can work with. And a script for a movie is quite different from a short story. You must expect certain revisions to be made."

"But how can you ask me to change the hero of the story? I know him, and I know what he's like. He's gentle and philosophical, and that's what makes the female character fall in love with him." She pushed away the cup of tea he had poured for her. "No, I don't want any." Bonita sat quietly, thinking about everything her grandmother had ever told her about her father.

He put the cup down and sat on the couch beside her. "He has to be drawn larger than life for movie audiences to accept him. He has to be more decisive and more manly."

"No!" Bonita cried out, standing up suddenly and remembering her father's dark eyes, his kind smile, and the slow pacing of his words. "I won't change him. You'll have to take him as he is."

She tried to recall more, but her father had been killed with her mother in an automobile accident when she was only seven years old, so her memories of her parents consisted almost entirely of short scenes—small snatches of everyday life.

She remembered her father lifting her onto a pony, and once driving a rattly truck while she sat next to him and listened to him explain his love for this pastoral countryside. She remembered her mother braiding her hair and tying green ribbons on the ends, making up some little sing-song verse to keep her quiet and still as she worked. And she remembered her mother's small birdlike hands—so like Bonita's own—as she shelled peas in the kitchen. Those brief but vivid snapshots, and nothing more, except what her grandmother had told her about her mother and father when they were young, about their falling in love and then getting married right in this very front parlor of Mrs. Langmeade's ranch house.

Her grandmother had told her the story in an effort to make her parents seem more real to her. And the characters had become so real that Bonita had put the story down on paper in a very convincing way.

Shaking herself from her reverie, Bonita contemplated the rude and uncaring man across from her who now wanted to take this fragile story and change it to suit his own violent style. Well, she would never let him tamper with these people who were so important to her.

"I'm sorry, Mr. McCaslin. But don't you see how important this story is to me, how personal? I will not allow you to turn a beautiful man into a crude or violent character."

"Sounds to me like you're in love with the man," Jordan McCaslin said with the hint of a sneer in his voice, indicating that to him being in love with someone was a symptom of weakness.

"Well, if I am, or if I was, it's none of your business, it has nothing to do with this film," she said, and wondered why this unsettling man was so capable of provoking her anger.

Alberta Langmeade came in with her basket of muffins. Her presence, and the sweet smell of the hot bread in the air, made the atmosphere more cozy at once. Alberta insisted Bonita have a cup of tea, passed the basket of muffins to Jordan McCaslin, who ate three, and all the time fired questions at their guest about the procedures in moviemaking. Bonita found the answers interesting and knew the information would be helpful in the weeks ahead, but she was delighted to have her grandmother be the one to flatter the insufferable Jordan McCaslin with the attention of questions, for she fully intended not to give him that satisfaction.

Suddenly Jordan McCaslin stood up and looked at his watch. "I have an appointment with a realtor at eleven o'clock, so I'd better get going. I want to find a house to rent while we're filming up here. I find hotels so impersonal, don't you?" he said to Bonita.

She nodded slightly, wondering with a restless longing whether she would ever have a chance to find out how she felt about hotels. So far she had never spent a night anywhere but in this house.

"Thank you for the tea, Mrs. Langmeade. May I call you Alberta?"

Bonita watched grimly as her grandmother fussed with the neckline of her simple, flowered housedress, trying to make herself look worthy of the honor of being on a first-name basis with a great movie producer.

"And Miss Langmeade, may I call you Bonita?" he asked with a mocking smile. "I will pick you up tomorrow morning and we'll take a look at some of the places you had in mind when you wrote the story."

"What a fascinating young man," her grandmother bubbled as soon as they heard the car pull away from their door. "I've read all about him in those movie magazines that Grace keeps at her beauty shop," she said. "Always taking this beautiful girl or that one to a movie premiere. He's the most eligible bachelor in Hollywood."

"Let me help you with those tea things, Grandmother."

"He has a very important job, for such a young man."

"Probably inherited his job from some relative."

"In a way, I guess you could say he did. I read that his father was a well-known director. But it's said he would have done well no matter who his father was. Has lots of drive they say, and a lot of talent, too."

"Well, we'll see," Bonita said with a sigh of doubt as she took the tray from her grandmother. "But so far he seems to be trying to take a completely wrong approach to my story."

"Now, Bonita, he didn't have to let you write the script, you know. He could have brought in some professional to adapt it and left you out of it completely. Before you came in, he said that he wanted to give you this chance at writing it."

"Well, that was before he met me," she said. "Or before he knew who I was."

"That ought to teach you not to run around in those terrible old clothes all the time." As they reached the kitchen and put all the tea things on the counter, Alberta reached over to give her granddaughter a healthy bear hug.

"Honey, this is a big opportunity for you. You're finally going to be exposed to a whole new world, and meet lots of new people. I know what a lonely life you've had, living here with just an old woman for company. When you were little, I was busy all the time trying to run the ranch. Then when we sold off all the animals because I wasn't well, I still didn't have much time and energy to give you. And when it was time for you to go off to college, I went and had that heart attack, and you wouldn't leave me."

"That wasn't why I stayed here. I'm happy here. I wanted to stay and work at my writing."

Alberta looked down at her granddaughter. "But one thing I'm glad I did for you. I talked you into sending your story to that magazine. Now just look at all the wonderful new things on the horizon for you because of that!"

"I guess so," Bonita said tentatively, burying her face in her grandmother's shoulder and suddenly wondering if she was prepared for the strife and uncertainty of this new world.

## CHAPTER TWO

The next morning Bonita drove the winding road out of the valley to the charming village of Carmel. It was still early enough in the morning that the main street was not yet full of tourists shopping and she easily found a parking place right in front of a quaint arcade of shops. She hurried down the curving cobblestone path, past the vine-covered windows of the candy kitchen and the brightly lighted toy store display until she came to the dress shop. She was surprised to find both halves of the Dutch door closed and locked so she put her face close to the window and peered past the mannequins. She could see there were no lights on inside. She started to leave when she heard a jangle of keys and turned to see her friend Marlene Webb strolling toward the shop with unhurried steps.

"Bonita, what are you doing here? You never come to buy clothes from me."

"I was afraid I wouldn't get to buy any today, either."

"Don't tell that old witch who owns the shop, please. She thinks we should open at nine on the dot but I can't see the point to it. Now that she doesn't come in every day, I figure I'll open up when I'm good and ready."

Bonita followed her inside and browsed through the confusing jumble of new styles and colors while

Marlene took her time setting up the shop for the day.

"Are you really here to buy, or just killing time while you dream up a new story?" Marlene asked as she carried two flowering plants to the doorway and placed them just outside.

"My grandmother has convinced me I don't have anything decent to wear, so I'm here under protest but I'm here to buy."

"You told me you sold a story to a magazine and to a movie studio, so spend a little of the money on yourself. That's what I'd do," Marlene said.

Bonita had picked out several outfits, and she went into a fitting room to try them on. She came out a moment later to stand in front of the full-length mirror in a pair of bright plaid pants with a matching top and immediately felt small and clownish beside her sleek blond friend who was leaning against a counter watching her critically.

"Plaid is a no-no for you, I guess we can see that," Marlene said, making a snap judgment. "You're so short you can't carry it off. But you do wear bright colors well with your dark hair. Try this." Marlene grabbed the nearest outfit and thrust it at Bonita, then turned careful attention to the rack of larger sizes.

"Now what shall I wear today?" she said to no one in particular. "I'm in a heather kind of mood, I think."

"Does the owner let you wear whatever you want from the shop?" Bonita asked, at last understanding why Marlene always appeared so stylish and well dressed. She noticed the lack of direct response to her question.

"I'm the best advertisement we have, aren't I?" Marlene said, holding a dress in front of her as she gazed at herself in the mirror.

"Bonita, everyone at the Little Theatre has been asking me when you're going to write us another play. I want you to write me a glamorous part this time, something really right for me. Are you working on anything?"

"I have a few ideas," she said, and escaped to the dressing room.

Though Marlene's comments on the clothes that Bonita tried on were brutally frank, and tossed off with a detached lack of interest, Bonita benefited from them, and in a short while she had picked out a beautiful suit of small black and white checks, with a green velvet vest, bright red slacks with a jacket, and a long dress for evening wear. When she brought them to the counter, Marlene was nowhere in sight.

"Well, what do you think?" Marlene asked as she dramatically stepped through the curtains of the largest dressing room wearing a pale gray jersey dress with a circular skirt that swung sensuously about her tall frame.

"It's beautiful on you, Marlene. But could you write up my sales check? I have an appointment this morning and I don't want to be late."

"Must be something important to set you off on such a buying spree. Something to do with the movie?"

"Why, yes, you're right. The man who is going to produce the movie is here in town and he wants me to take him on a tour of the area today."

"What? The producer himself? Why didn't you tell me? You need something very special to wear today. Let me see." She started to wander away from the counter, suddenly very interested in getting involved with Bonita's choices.

"No, there really isn't time. These will be fine."

"Who is this producer? You haven't told me his name."

"Jordan McCaslin."

"The head of Magnet Studios? *That* Jordan McCaslin! He's here in town right now?" Marlene was so impressed that the words tumbled out of her mouth with none of the slow husky phrasing she usually affected.

She left the clothes rack to gaze out the front window of the shop, deep in thought. "I know who he is. I've seen pictures of him. He has a huge home in Beverly Hills with a tennis court, and all the famous people come to play tennis with him. And the women in his life!" She turned around slowly. "Oh, Bonita, be careful of him. He's a professional Lothario."

She came to stand close to Bonita, and put her arm around her shoulder so that Bonita felt like a small, incompetent person in need of her tall friend's protection.

"This is the big time, and you're not ready for it. You can't handle a man like that. They say he's a real barracuda."

"From what I've seen, that description fits him rather nicely."

"You must keep your distance, don't let him try to make you one of his conquests."

"Marlene, this is a purely business relationship."

"Well, see that you keep it that way. He's a man not to be trusted. Believe me, as your friend I'm warning you."

"I am in a hurry, Marlene. Could you please ring up this sale?"

Marlene worked over the sales book and cash register at her maddeningly slow pace, and kept stopping to quiz Bonita on every detail of the important man's visit. At last the business transaction was completed and Bonita rushed for the door. Marlene followed her and leaned in the doorway as if she had all day to banter.

"By the way, how's that big hunk of man you spend so much time with?" Marlene asked.

"You mean Brad Stark?" Bonita asked with surprise.

"Yes. He never has much to say, but he sure looks

good flexing his muscles while he's standing around not saying it."

"Brad is just a neighbor. I ride his horses once in a while. We really don't spend that much time together."

"I thought that maybe at last you'd found yourself a boyfriend."

"Oh, no, Marlene. No new gossip for you from my direction. When there is, I'll let you know."

"Don't you worry. I'll keep in touch."

Later that morning it was a uniformed chauffeur who came to the door to call for Bonita. When she went outside with him, she was surprised to see that the rental car Jordan had been driving the day before had been replaced by a long sleek limousine. Apparently he had decided he was too important a person to be bothered any further by the hazards of driving on country roads.

Bonita had never been inside a limousine before, and as the driver held the door for her, she tried to stifle her feelings of wonder and not look too impressed. The backseat was huge, and upholstered in a lush gray velours. Taking up easily half of the space was Jordan McCaslin, his long legs stretched in front of him as he studied a leather notebook. His hair was catching the sun through the car window, and the lighter strands stood out like polished silver against the dark tan of his skin. He didn't bother with any social amenities but came right to the point as soon as she was seated next to him.

"Looking over this scene breakdown I've made I can see most of our filming will be done at the heroine's home. Now, we'll need a ranch with a large horse paddock area, and of course an old house. Can you think of anyplace . . ."

"Of course the perfect place would be Brad Stark's

place right next door. That's what I was thinking of when I wrote the description."

Jordan McCaslin put the book down and looked at her for the first time. She adjusted the jacket of her new red pants outfit nervously as he studied her, but he was obviously not the type to take notice of new clothes.

"Next door, you say?"

"Yes, you can walk right across that field there and get to Brad's place. But we'll have to drive down the road and out onto the highway to his main gate." She leaned forward, aiming her words to the driver by way of instructions.

As they drove past the part of the fence that the car had splintered the day before, Bonita talked quickly so that neither she nor the man sitting deep in thought beside her would be reminded of what had happened there.

"I think you'll agree this will be the perfect location for the movie. And I know Brad will be glad to cooperate."

"Will he?"

"He's only owned the place a few years. He came up here from central California with money to invest and bought the Beasley ranch. He's put a lot of money into his horses and barn, but the house is still just as it was fifty years ago."

Bonita joined Jordan McCaslin's quiet mood as she remembered how unhappy she'd been to see her mother's home sold to a stranger. But when Grandfather Beasley died and Bonita inherited the ranch, there had been nothing to do but put it up for sale, for she and her grandmother already had more land than they could properly take care of. Then she had met the new owner, and they had become good friends, and it seemed right to see the old ranch next door revitalized.

Brad came loping toward their car from his barn

as soon as they came to a stop in the open grassy field in the middle of his property. He pulled off his cowboy hat and wiped his forehead as he circled the car.

"Wow, that's some big fancy car you're riding in nowadays, Bonita. Aren't you some lady of style!" He grinned expansively at her and then turned to greet Jordan McCaslin.

"Hi there, I'm Brad Stark."

"Mr. Stark, I'm Jordan McCaslin of Magnet Studios. I'm going to be producing a movie in this area and Bonita tells me you would be willing to let me look over your ranch."

"Sure, glad to give you a tour. It isn't a very showy place. I haven't had time to fix it up very much."

"We're looking for a movie location, not a spot for a barn dance," McCaslin said curtly.

"Well, let me show you around," Brad said.

"That won't be necessary. If you'll step out of my way I'll look around on my own to see if it suits my requirements and we'll forget the guided tour."

He put his notebook under his arm and strode away from them. Brad and Bonita leaned against the car and watched him as he walked between the house and the barn, studying the buildings from every possible angle and stopping to pace off distances and study the vistas of green hills in the background. From time to time he took a round black object from his pocket and peered through it as if it were a short telescope.

Brad let out a low whistle as he put his hat back on and then said to Bonita, "Now there's a man who seems to know exactly what he wants. How are you getting along with the great Hollywood producer?"

"Not very well," she said. "What he wants is to do everything his way. He seems to forget that I wrote the story and that I know how it should be done."

Brad leaned toward Bonita and grabbed her upper

arms awkwardly in his heavy workman's hands. "If there's anything I can do to help you, just let me know. If using my ranch will help your story, you just tell me and I'll cooperate. But if you don't want those movie people here, say the word and I'll run and get my shotgun and send him packing right now."

Bonita laughed as she looked up into Brad's kind eyes. His cowboy boots and hat made him appear taller than he actually was, and his muscular shoulders seemed to strain through the fabric of his shirt so that he seemed powerful enough to move mountains for Bonita if it were necessary.

"Of course I want them to use your ranch. It's perfect," she said, and then the sound of a harshly intruding voice just behind her made her pull herself quickly from Brad's grip.

"How about letting me be the judge of that. I've had a little more experience at making movies," Jordan McCaslin said as he finished writing something in his leather notebook and closed it with a snap. He held the black device to his eye for one more scan of the horizon.

"I can't figure out what that thing is you're looking through," Brad said.

"Of course you can't. I'm sure you've never seen one before. It's a lens. I'm checking camera angles to make sure we can get those hills in the background of all our long shots. I've never seen anything like them, they're like velvet. If we do some early-morning filming when the sun is at a slant, we should get a back-light effect that will be spectacular." He was almost talking to himself, and his hypnotic voice trailed off until it was barely audible as he studied the surroundings.

"You want to see the inside of the house?" Brad asked.

"Whatever for? I've seen all I need to see," Jordan

answered, putting the lens back into a leather case and slipping it into the pocket of his heavy white cardigan.

"Well, what do you think? Are you going to use my humble home for your movie?"

"Mr. Stark, you're not aware of what is involved. Do you realize that if we decide to film here there will be hundreds of technicians and truckloads of equipment on your property for days, maybe weeks? It will cause quite an interruption in your work."

"Don't worry about that. I'll put up with anything to make Bonita's movie a success."

Bonita winced as she wondered whether Jordan would correct Brad and point out that it was now his movie, not Bonita's.

"I'll send my art director over here tomorrow to look around some more and take some photographs. He can show you our legal forms and explain our standard leasing arrangements. But in the meantime I think you should consider this carefully. I have to be honest with you and tell you that we sometimes make a mess of a place before we're through."

"You sound like you're trying to talk him out of it," Bonita snapped.

"I'm trying to prevent any misunderstandings," he said slowly, turning to Bonita with a patient sigh as if he were bored with having to explain himself to her.

Just then Brad's housekeeper, Anna, came rushing toward them from the house.

"Mr. Stark, I have a telephone message for Miss Bonita. Her grandmother just called."

"What did she want?" Bonita asked.

"Mrs. Langmeade says you're to be sure and invite your guest to dinner tonight, Miss Bonita. And Mr. Stark, she wants you to go on over there to her house for dinner tonight, too."

Bonita sighed with exasperation. Her grandmother

had not consulted her about this and now the invitation had been made before she could stop it.

"That sounds great," Brad said enthusiastically. "Now Mr. McCaslin will have a chance to explain to me some more about how he plans to take apart my place."

"I haven't made any commitment that this is the ranch we'll be using," Jordan said to Brad so sharply that Bonita turned to stare up into his piercing eyes. "I'll be looking over other places all day today."

Luckily Brad did not seem bothered by Jordan McCaslin's abrasive personality, but Bonita felt obliged to insert some good manners into the conversation.

"Will you accept my grandmother's invitation?" she asked Jordan with a hesitant sigh.

"With pleasure. I'll be there about seven." He lifted a tanned wrist to look at his watch. "Well, I've got to get going. There's still the Carmel Mission to look over and I want to see some beach locations."

Bonita's eyes widened with interest as she envisioned showing him the famous Seventeen-Mile Drive that curved through wooded areas and along what she was sure was the most beautiful coastline in the world.

"You're used to walking home from here right through that field, didn't you say, Bonita? So, I'll leave you here and be on my way. I'll see you both tonight." And with that Jordan McCaslin stepped into his limousine and closed the door, leaving Bonita to stand with a disgusted look on her face as the car drove off down the ranch road toward the highway.

"What an insufferable man," she exclaimed. "I don't know why he treated you so rudely."

"Now, honey," Brad answered Bonita. "He's just one of those high-pressured big-city types you're not used to. Just stay out of his way and he won't bother you. After a few months this will all be over and we can return to normal. Do you want me to walk you home?"

37

"No, you have work to do. I'll see you tonight."

As Bonita walked across the field she wondered what had ever made her grandmother think of inviting the movie producer to a mundane ranch house meal. As soon as she came in the kitchen door, she saw that preparations were underway. Her grandmother had just put the top crust on an apple pie and was placing it in the oven.

"Bonita, I'm sure you think I've lost my mind, inviting Mr. McCaslin to dinner on such short notice." She stood up and pushed a strand of gray hair in place behind her ear. "It had just never occurred to me that we should show that young man some hospitality. Then your friend Marlene Webb called up and asked me what we were doing to entertain Mr. McCaslin. Well, I decided right on the spot to have a dinner party. Marlene was just thrilled to death."

Bonita dropped the leftover apple slice she had just picked up to snack on.

"Marlene is coming, too?"

"It was practically her idea. I couldn't leave her out of it, with her so interested in Hollywood and all."

"You're not supposed to work so hard, this is too much for you," Bonita protested.

"I haven't had so much fun in years." Alberta turned back to her work at the kitchen counter, humming happily to herself at the unusual excitement in the air.

"Let me help you then."

"You can set the table for me while I get a ham ready to bake."

Bonita went into the dining room and took down the silver chest, wondering glumly to herself why she couldn't feel the same enthusiasm for another confrontation with the smug superiority of Jordan McCaslin.

That evening after all the guests had assembled in Alberta Langmeade's old-fashioned living room, Bonita stepped aside for a moment to prepare a tray of glasses and a decanter of sherry. So far, Jordan McCaslin had behaved like a subdued child who'd been sent to a party by his mother with dire warnings to be polite and charming. He had brought Alberta a beautifully wrapped bottle of wine as a gift, and he had even spoken civilly to Brad for the first time. But Bonita had the tense feeling that at any moment he would burst through the pleasant veneer and again reveal his true nature.

Bonita noticed that Marlene Webb had insisted that Jordan sit beside her on the small couch, and at the moment she was curving herself close to him in earnest conversation. She interrupted her dialogue to take the glass offered her.

"Why, Bonita. How quaint of you to serve sherry, of all things, before dinner. I was just telling Jordan about our Little Theatre here in Carmel. Tell him about the wonderful part you wrote for me in your play last year."

"It was the story of a crippled girl who wants to learn to paint, and the famous artist who helps her."

"A love story, no doubt," Jordan said, and Bonita was hurt by the derisive tone in his voice.

"Well, yes, it was. Would you care for a glass of sherry? I'm sure you're used to champagne, but we're just simple ranch people here in the valley."

Jordan stood up to take a glass from the tray, and when he spoke to her his words were so quiet that she was sure even Marlene could not hear them. "Aren't you being a bit of a snob?"

"I beg your pardon?"

"You're the one who seems to feel this sherry is not quite good enough. I happen to think it's perfect." And then he raised his glass on high and turned to face the rest of the group. Bonita was left standing with a burst of color in her cheeks, still reeling from his insult.

"When everyone has a glass, I'd like to propose a toast."

Mrs. Langmeade and Brad hurried to take theirs, and Bonita took one and placed the tray back on the sideboard.

"To our author, once known only in this valley, and soon to be known to the world."

With Jordan's words all the attention in the room was directed toward Bonita, and she struggled to regain her composure as everyone turned to stare at her. Bonita was sure that Jordan had planned it this way. First the low-pitched insult, then the praise at a moment when she was too disconcerted to respond properly. She turned away, adjusting the embroidered cuffs that edged the long sleeves of her new green dress to hide her embarrassment. Marlene saved her by diverting the attention back to herself.

"I'm just sorry, Jordan, that our Little Theatre group doesn't have a production before the footlights right now so that you could come and see me onstage. I've been acting now for four years, ever since Bonita and I graduated from high school. I must be Bonita's good luck talisman. She always *insists* that I appear in her plays, even when she thinks up some grim character with a bad leg for me to play."

Bonita smiled indulgently at her friend's exaggeration. It was pure coincidence that Marlene had appeared in the three plays that Bonita had written for the acting group.

Jordan sat down again so that he could concentrate completely on Marlene's slowly delivered, well-modulated words. There was a languorous quality to the girl, accented by the alluring softness of the jersey dress she had modeled for Bonita in the morning and was still wearing, that obviously appealed to Jordan McCaslin.

Bonita was chatting with Brad in front of the fireplace a few minutes later when she noticed Jordan giving her an irritated look, and then heard him say to Marlene, "All right. If Bonita insisted upon it then I'll arrange a screen test for you. But I can't promise you a part in this picture even if you are an experienced actress. There is a small role of a schoolteacher who serves as a go-between for our young lovers, and it hasn't been cast yet. But we'll have to take a look at how you come across on camera."

Bonita was horrified. She would never have considered making any such suggestion that Marlene be tested for a part in the film. But apparently Marlene had seen a way to use a small white lie and her friendship with Bonita to get what she wanted.

Marlene was looking at Jordan McCaslin as if she were a dieter watching a cake decorator through a bakery window. Bonita frowned unconsciously, wondering for a moment if Marlene was going to jump right into his lap and cover his face with traces of her pale peach lipstick, for her grateful look promised at least that much.

Just then Alberta Langmeade announced dinner, and Jordan McCaslin was quick to stand up and offer her his arm and escort her to the table.

"I guess that leaves me with just the two most beautiful young girls in this valley to take to the dining room," Brad laughed as he offered Marlene and Bonita his arms.

As Jordan seated Mrs. Langmeade, she asked him, "Have you found all your locations for the picture?"

"Too many," he said. "This area has enough picturesque backgrounds for my next ten pictures. By the way, Alberta, if we use Mr. Stark's ranch we may want to do some filming here on your property. As the story describes, the young hero cleverly arranged to meet his love secretly by walking to her ranch on a path through the field."

"Oh, yeah?" Brad said good naturedly, a biscuit halfway to his mouth.

For no reason at all Jordan stopped his story to scowl at Brad, as if to reprimand him for even the slightest interruption. "Most of the action takes place over there, but I may want a dolly shot across the field to show how they meet. Would you be willing to let me use your place?"

"Willing?" Alberta bubbled. "Why, I'd just love that. Then I can see just how a movie is made."

"The only thing I haven't lined up yet is a place to use as our base camp. I need somewhere to park all our trucks and trailers and a building for our film editing and equipment. As I figure it, we'll be shooting up here for several weeks."

"What about using our place for that, too?" Alberta offered. "Our big barn is all cleaned out. Since we got rid of our horses, it's just stood empty. And there is certainly enough room around here to park all your vehicles."

"Grandmother, I'm sure he needs more facilities than we have to offer."

"No, you're wrong Bonita. If your grandmother is willing to put up with all the noise and confusion, this would be the ideal spot. A barn is just what I was thinking of using."

"Does that mean you've decided to use my ranch?" Brad asked.

"Unfortunately, I don't think I have any choice. If we're going to be authentic, then wherever possible we should use the actual places Bonita had in mind when she wrote her story," Jordan said, and he looked at Bonita across the flickering candle on the table between them.

Bonita thought she could see every leap and twist of the flame reflected in his light eyes as he studied her, apparently waiting for a reaction. She busied herself with passing the basket of biscuits around the table so she wouldn't have to acknowledge his attempt to appease her.

She supposed she should be grateful that he was filming the story in Carmel. She knew many producers preferred to save expenses by shooting their films in Hollywood. He had very correctly observed that the Carmel Valley was like one of the characters in her story, and he had accepted her suggestion that he use the actual ranch where the story took place. Now if she could just keep him from savagely twisting her story by changing the characters as he seemed determined to do!

"What? I'm sorry. I didn't hear what you said," Bonita suddenly blurted, realizing she had drifted far away from the dinner-table conversation.

Marlene slowly repeated her words, obviously irritated over Bonita's lack of attention. "Don't you think Jordan's game sounds like fun?"

"What game?"

"I merely suggested that each of you tell me your favorite movie. I'm always interested in hearing what people outside the movie business remember as their all-time favorite films," Jordan said.

Bonita realized from the cynical look of amusement on Jordan's face that it was more than mere curiosity that had caused him to propose the game. She sensed that this was some sort of psychological trap he was setting, and she had no desire to step into it.

"I have no trouble there, young man," Alberta said. "There has only been one great movie ever made and that was *Gone With the Wind*. My late husband and I went to see that picture four times, and we both cried ourselves silly every time and loved every minute of it."

"A beautiful film," Jordan agreed and she glowed under his approval. "Brad, what about you? Do you ever go to the movies?" Jordan asked.

"I mostly see them on television. It's hard to remember which ones I've really liked. Let's see, there was *The Big Country,* and *Butch Cassidy and the Sundance*

*Kid,* and, oh yes, I liked *Bridge on the River Kwai.*"

"Action pictures, Westerns. That's no surprise," Jordan said, making a quick judgment of Brad's taste.

"Being an actress, I think I look for performances," Marlene said. "I will always remember Bette Davis in *All About Eve.* And, of course, Vivien Leigh in *A Streetcar Named Desire,* and I think Elizabeth Taylor's best performance was Maggie in *Cat on a Hot Tin Roof.*"

"So you are a Tennessee Williams fan," Jordan said, nodding his head knowingly, as if there was a heavy implication to his words. Bonita stood up quickly to begin clearing the dinner plates.

"It's your turn, Bonita," Marlene said. "Can't you forget practising your housewifery for a minute and keep the game going?"

"I think while I'm busy we should hear from the Hollywood expert himself," she said, hoping her turn would be forgotten in everyone's eagerness to hear Jordan speak his preferences. "After all, he proposed the game."

"All right. I'm not worried about what my choices will reveal about myself. I remember the films that have influenced film making. There was *Citizen Kane, On the Waterfront, Blow Up, Easy Rider, Nashville,* and one my father directed that few people remember, *Three for Victory,* during the war."

"Why didn't you become a director like your father?" Alberta asked.

"I've tried it," he said. "But I like to be in control of the whole project, even watching over the director's shoulder. On this picture coming up I'm using a very young director whose experience has mainly been in television. So I'll be backstopping him all along the way."

As Bonita placed a dessert plate in front of each person, she watched Jordan and marveled at how his taut energy had taken charge of the entire conversation. *He does want to control things*, she thought. Perhaps that's what has made him such a good producer, his attention to every detail and his desire to implant his choices on every phase of his pictures. But such selfish obstinance would make him a difficult person to get along with personally, and she could see rough days ahead in working with him.

"Now that you're back with us, perhaps you'll tell us your choices," Jordan said, ignoring the piece of pie in front of him and leaning forward on his elbows, watching her ominously.

"Well, I've liked all different types of pictures. For musicals I'd have to say *Gigi*. The best epic picture I've seen was *Doctor Zhivago*. My favorite comedy, and I watch it on television all the time, is *It Happened One Night*." She considered her choices carefully, noticing that Jordan had not taken his eyes off her.

"Any foreign films?" he asked.

"I liked *The Umbrellas of Cherbourg*," she said. "Oh, and for old classics I'd have to say *Philadelphia Story*."

"All you've left out is *Love Story*," Jordan said with a sarcastic grin as he picked up his fork.

"What do you mean?"

"Well, you said you liked different kinds of pictures but every one you mentioned was a love story. You don't seem to consider a picture good unless it is heavily loaded with emotion."

"Is that wrong?"

"Not wrong, just revealing," he said, dismissing her choices with his quick verdict. Bonita thought back over the titles he'd mentioned and realized there was not a love story in the group, but she was afraid to mention that she thought his choices just as revealing as her own. He obviously thought her sentimental and naive, and he would see his own preferences for downbeat action and conflict stories as the more worldly approach.

As everyone left the table Bonita stayed behind to help her grandmother set up a tray of coffee cups. Marlene was quick to fall in step beside Jordan on the way into the living room and Bonita could hear her begin a conversation which would be sure to interest him.

"I've read Bonita's story in the magazine and I think you can turn it into a beautiful film when you give it your special touch. You know, I have a special interpretation of the story that you might be interested in hearing. True, it's just a simple love story, but it has a quality of reality about it which ... "

Bonita wondered as the conversation ebbed out of her hearing if Marlene could have guessed that the story was about her own mother and father. She hoped that wasn't what Marlene was going to tell him, for she couldn't face any more of his mockery.

"Brad, could you carry this heavy tray for us?" Alberta asked.

"Sure, be glad to."

"Wait, we need the sugar and cream," Alberta said, hurrying back toward the kitchen.

"*Star Wars*," Brad said suddenly, staring at Bonita but not seeing her.

"What?"

"I forgot to name *Star Wars*. I loved that picture. And talking about old pictures, how come no one named *High Noon*?"

"Oh, Brad," Bonita laughed. "The game is over. Jordan McCaslin has had his fun. He now thinks he knows all about our simple, common tastes in films. Now let's leave the subject of Hollywood."

"I thought you were interested in that subject," Brad said.

"Well, I'm not," she answered with a vehemence that surprised her.

"I've always had the feeling you want to know more about exciting places like Hollywood, and go to those kind of places. I don't think you're really a country girl at heart, Bonita."

"I love it here, and I want to stay here always, doing just what I'm doing. Sure, I get restless now and then, and I want to meet new people. But this is my home," she said, sweeping her arm around the dining room but taking in the entire valley with her thought.

"But don't you get lonely, just staying here with your grandmother, writing all the time? I mean, trotting around on my land on my horses, that's enough for me. But you seem like a girl that really wants to go galloping."

Bonita stopped to consider his question carefully, surprised at Brad's intuition. Maybe she had talked to him more frankly than she had realized during their years of friendship. He was, after all, the only person her age that she saw regularly. Before she could decide on a true answer to his question, her grandmother came into the room.

"All right, children. Everything's ready. Shall we go into the living room?"

"How much longer do you plan to stay in Carmel, Mr. McCaslin?" Brad asked as they entered the living room, interrupting Marlene's conversation and getting a cold glare from her as a result.

Jordan looked at his watch. "As a matter of fact, I have to be in my office tomorrow morning. My pilot's waiting at the airport to take me back tonight. So if you will all excuse me, I won't stay for coffee."

Everyone stood up and began talking at once, saying the things people always say at the end of a pleasant evening. Bonita was startled amid the mumble of voices to hear the unmistakable husky drawl of Jordan McCaslin close to her ear.

"Come with me to the car," he said and she began to move at his command.

Jordan turned and raised his hand to the others in the room almost as if he were offering the benediction.

47

"Your dinner was delightful, Alberta. Thank you for the opportunity to get to know all of you."

"I'm just so glad I thought of it, aren't you?" Marlene said to Alberta, her voice raised loudly enough that Jordan would be sure to hear as he guided Bonita out the door with him.

Outside, the night was surprisingly cold, and Bonita shivered as she stepped onto the porch and looked up into the dark sky brightened with a clear sparkling of stars.

"You're cold. I'm sorry, I didn't think of that. I have to talk to you for a moment." He removed his soft suede jacket and draped it around her shoulders.

"I won't be back here for a while, so I have to get your answer tonight on this script business. Do you want the assignment to write the final draft for me, or not? If you're not willing to rewrite it the way I've suggested, then I'll have to hire an experienced professional screenwriter in Hollywood to take it to the shooting script version."

Bonita was upset to think that a complete stranger might be brought in to hack away at her cherished pages. And yet she was reluctant to revise it just to suit Jordan McCaslin's presumptuous commands. "I don't know. The changes you're asking for are . . ."

"Believe me, I understand what you're going through. But once you give it a try you'll find that making the revisions I've asked for won't hurt too much."

Jordan's voice was more gently persuasive than she'd ever heard it before. Almost without realizing it she fell in step with his friendly mood.

"I'd like to try. I know you're offering me an opportunity that I should appreciate."

Bonita knew that she would have to try to approach this job dispassionately, that she would have to force herself to cut into her story with the cold dispatch of an uninvolved professional. But could she, when the story meant so much to her?

She walked beside him down the front steps and along the driveway toward the car. The jacket around her shoulders had not yet warmed her, and she made a soft shuddering sound as she exhaled a steamy breath of air into the cold night. Jordan seemed to notice and without a word he put his arm around her and bunched the jacket closer to her body.

There was something very safe about being protected in Jordan McCaslin's hold, and Bonita found that she was comfortable with him for the first time since their embarrassing first encounter. They walked slowly and silently together, his high wide shoulders slanted down toward her tiny ones dwarfed in his coat. She felt that as long as she was in the custody of this intense and decisive man she was guarded against the cold air around her as well as any other threat.

When they were a few feet from the car, he stopped and turned her toward him. Putting his arms around her, he hugged her so close to him that she was sure she could feel the special vitality that energized him flowing through his body and warming her. She had to remind herself that he was merely keeping her warm, that his embrace was meaningless, but he held her for such a long time, saying nothing, that she soon forgot, and she turned her head to rest it comfortably on the smooth silk of his tie. Her ear was so close to his chest that his voice when he spoke again sounded like the soft rumble of distant thunder.

"Mmm. You smell good," he said. "I thought I could identify every perfume in the world, but I can't tell what you've dabbed behind your ears."

"It's not perfume . . ." she started, but stopped with a frightened feeling of alarm as she felt his warm lips searching her cheeks and neck for the scent. Marlene had warned her of his reputation as a lover, and she realized she was letting him work his special magic on her, but she was powerless to stop him, for her mind was reeling with confusing questions. Why had his attitude toward her so suddenly changed? And why was she responding to his new and more gentle approach when she knew it was not sincere?

"It's not just behind your ears, it's everywhere," he laughed huskily close to her face. "I'll bet it's just the scent of good soap and fresh clean air. I'm not used to an outdoor girl like you."

Bonita wondered how much longer she could stand the proximity of such an intoxicating man. She was already aware of disturbing new emotions taking control of her, emotions she had only imagined before when she had identified with the heroines of exciting love stories. But she had no time to luxuriate in the wild new sensations, for Jordan McCaslin abruptly drew the curtain on the scene she was enjoying. He pulled away from her, and as the cold air rushed between them it awakened her lulled senses with a sharp thrust.

"I know that you'll see I'm right about your story when you stop being so suspicious of me," he said, suddenly businesslike again. "Trust me, and believe that I don't want to ruin your story."

Bonita stared up at him, feeling so betrayed that she was sure he must be able to see in her face that whatever trust he had inspired in her a moment before he had now dissolved with his quick return to the topic of scriptwriting.

He obviously thought he could use his talent for romance to win over a simple star-struck farm girl to his ways with one quick embrace, and she knew at once that whatever haven she thought she'd found in his arms was a cruel deception. He was intent upon convincing her to write the script his way. His one-track mind was dedicated to seeing that he got what he wanted, and he used any means to accomplish that goal. All she wanted to do was run away from him, back to the warm hearth and the bright lights inside the house.

He opened the car door and started to step inside, saying, "I'll need your revised script in four weeks, so you have a lot of work to do," and his crisply efficient words put the final icy glaze on Bonita's heart. She resolved never to let this ruthless man close enough to bewitch her again.

"Don't forget your coat," she said, thrusting it into the car after him, and she turned to run up the driveway to the comfort of the house as fast as possible, wishing she would never have to set foot outside its secure boundaries again in her life.

## CHAPTER THREE

"Is that you, Bonita? Back already?"

"Yes, Grandmother. I'll bring the mail up to you in just a minute," Bonita called up the stairs as she stopped to take off her windbreaker.

"Anything from Magnet Studios?"

"No," Bonita smiled, only slightly perturbed at the question she'd heard every day this week.

"I just don't understand why you haven't had a letter from Jordan McCaslin. When did you mail him your new draft of the script?" Alberta asked as she came down the stairs.

"Grandmother, this is your rest time. You belong upstairs in bed."

"It's harder on my heart to sit and mope in my room

than it is to be up and about. Now tell me when you mailed him your script."

"Two weeks ago, but I'm not waiting to hear from him."

"You're not waiting for a letter? Then why have you taken to walking to the mailbox every afternoon? It's gotten to be such a habit that Lark comes barking for you now when he hears the mailman's truck down on the highway."

"I am curious, of course. I tried to make the changes he asked for and I wonder if they satisfied him."

"If he hasn't written to complain, then I think you can figure he's happy with your script."

Bonita had found that making some small changes in her story line had been, as Jordan had predicted, easier than she'd expected. As she wrote the script she found herself unconsciously adding touches of assertion to her characters, and scenes with greater conflict than had been in her first draft.

Her work had given her an odd kind of respect for Jordan McCaslin's talents, for she could see in the finished manuscript a movie rather than a lyric story. She had remained faithful throughout to what she remembered of her father's personality, but she had come to realize, as she was writing, that as his daughter she had probably only seen one side of him, the gentleness he would show to a little girl, and she had tried to make him more forceful in his interactions with the characters in the story.

At first she wondered why the producer had not responded to the changes he knew she had been so reluctant to try. Didn't he want to gloat over the fact that he had won her over with just a few minutes of his well-practiced romantic ardor? Surely he was congratulating himself on another stunning performance. But as the days passed with no letter from Hollywood, she had begun to realize that her changes were probably not sufficient, and that he was no doubt unhappy with her script. She could picture him hard at work in Hollywood, trying to figure out how to add a shoot-out or a troop of uniformed combat soldiers to the script, taking time out only to escort some famous starlet to a premiere or a party.

Bonita put on the big round glasses she wore for reading and went into the living room with the new magazines that had come in the mail, while Alberta went to her desk by the window to open the bills. After a few quiet minutes they both heard a car in the driveway.

"Who could that be coming for a visit?" Alberta asked, craning her neck. "Why, it's your friend Marlene. I thought she worked at that dress shop all day."

"She works only when it doesn't interfere with what else she wants to do," Bonita said with a laugh. "I've known her to close up the place in the middle of a summer Saturday just to go have her hair styled."

As she went to the door, Bonita wondered what had prompted this display of friendliness from Marlene. She hoped the theatre group had not sent her to make another appeal to Bonita to write a play for them, for she was physically exhausted after a month of hard work on the movie script. Marlene had been calling her every few days lately, just to check up on her progress with her writing and to remind her about the play.

"The town is certainly buzzing with the news," Marlene said without bothering to go through the nuisance of greeting Bonita or her grandmother. "Every person who's come into the shop today has been talking about the same thing. This is the most excitement I've seen around here since my play at the Little Theatre was held over for an extra weekend," she drawled, stretching out her story for maximum effect.

"What's going on?" Bonita asked.

"Well, if you'd get out of the house more and quit

acting like a bookworm, you'd get in on all the local news," Marlene said.

Bonita removed her glasses and offered Marlene a seat, losing all interest in Marlene's suspenseful story now that she knew it was just another of her tidbits of local gossip, always told with great style and relish and always totally unimportant.

"I sold four dresses just this morning for the same party. All the local big shots have been invited, and you ought to see how thrilled they are to be meeting the movie people." She was looking at Bonita attentively, apparently watching her for some telltale reaction that would indicate if Bonita already knew more about this than she did.

"What movie people?" Alberta turned on her desk chair to ask.

"Just Jordan McCaslin, that's all. And everyone he's brought with him."

"Jordan McCaslin is back in town?" Bonita asked, unable to mask her surprise.

"Why yes, didn't you know, Bonita?" Marlene said, pouting with an elaborate display of surprise. "He's rented that two-acre Perkins estate out there just past the Del Monte Lodge on the Seventeen-Mile Drive. You know, Addie Perkins was just in the shop buying more clothes before she left on her annual jaunt to Europe. Has she ever put on weight! And she was telling me that she'd leased her house out for a few months. Guess the poor old thing needs a little injection of money to make that inheritance last until she finds another husband."

"And Jordan McCaslin is moving into her house?" Bonita asked when she was able to speak.

"He's all moved in. I suppose you'll be hearing from him once he gets this party for all the important people over with and settles down to work," Marlene said, now as content as a well-fed kitten, and no longer interested in the conversation.

him and grabbed the expensive em-
dkerchief from his hands and began
n at her wet blouse and jeans.
gardener I wanted the automatic sprin-
it off," he said, "but he kept telling me
tter, that this wasn't Beverly Hills where
n the lawn." He had to force himself to
ords between subsiding laughter.
ver seen him let himself go and relax
re amusement, his head thrown back so
worn longer than most of the men she
softly across his shirt collar. She won-
why she had to be the one to provide
fun.
aid, taking her by the hand and leading
box on one wall of the patio where an
ical system controlled the sprinklers. He
h or two and the sprinklers shut off.
four o'clock they go on for fifteen min-

o stare down at her, ignoring the fact
ung her head his suit was spotted with
r from her hair.
ally think I would turn the sprinklers

was I supposed to think?"
enough that you never got your invita-
ty. Of course you're supposed to be here.
ching for you, there are some special
want you to meet."
holding her hand, and he led her into
a side door. She was relieved to see
a bedroom where there were no guests.
up in this towel. I'm going to get some
e to take a look at you."
over to the door and she heard him
ne just outside. "Send Vic and Charlotte

Bonita understood that Marlene had come in the guise of giving information, while actually she had come to find out whether Bonita had heard from Jordan yet. Bonita knew that the confused surprise she felt was written plainly enough on her face for Marlene to read it clearly, for she had never been any good at covering up her feelings.

"I guess I could have just called you to tell you about this," Marlene said as she stood up to leave. "But you know how I love sharing this exciting time with you, dear. I'll come by tomorrow on my way home from the shop and bring you a couple of dresses to try on. You'll need decent clothes now that the movie company is here, and I'm so glad to be available to help you."

"Thank you, Marlene, but I have plenty now."

"Oh, it's no trouble. See you tomorrow," Marlene said, going down the front steps with a more lively spring to her step than Bonita had ever seen before.

"Why that terrible man. Here I am waiting for some word from him about the script, and he moves into his house not five miles away and doesn't even give me a call."

"He's probably been busy with other matters," her grandmother said soothingly, and Bonita was grateful that her grandmother wasn't the type to gloat, now that she had admitted her grandmother's suspicions about her anxious trips to the mailbox were right.

"I'm going to go see him right this minute. Where did Marlene say he was staying?"

"Out at that big home right on the water at Pebble Beach, beyond Pescadero Point. You remember when that rich widow bought it a couple of years ago? It's a beautiful place."

Within ten minutes Bonita was entering the Seventeen-Mile Drive at the Carmel gate and driving the familiar winding road in her old Ford convertible. Her mind was in such a state of agitation that she didn't even notice the uniquely bitter scent of the cypress forest around her. Usually she would have stopped to put the top down on such a sunny day so that she could savor every bit of the beauty this verdant area had to offer, but today all she had on her mind was finding Jordan McCaslin and making him tell her what he thought of her script.

The guard at the gate had given her good directions to the Perkins estate, but she'd been confused when he looked at her casual jeans outfit and said, "Guess you don't need an invitation, you'll be going in the back door to help the caterers."

Then when she pulled up in front of the rambling Spanish-style mansion set before the awesome backdrop of the Pacific Ocean she realized that the party Marlene had mentioned was already in progress. She saw one well-dressed couple present a white engraved card to the maid at the front door and go right inside. Since she had not received an invitation to the party, she was sure she wouldn't be admitted. But she was not going to give up now that she had come so far.

The gate guard had given her a good idea. She parked her car and headed around the side of the house. She could hear music playing inside, and the sound of voices and tinkling glassware, but she couldn't find the service entrance. She took a well-manicured path through a cutting garden and came out on the broad back lawn of the house facing the ocean.

She had never visited any of the huge mansions that fronted on this bit of coastline near the prestigious Del Monte Lodge. Wealthy people came from all over the world to retire here and enjoy all the golf courses and the elegant social life.

She saw a hexagonal gazebo out on the edge of the cliff overlooking the water, and she started to walk toward it. She was curious to see the ocean from a in here right away, will you? And tell them to bring their work kits."

He closed the door again, shutting out the babble of the party and looking at her critically. "You can't come out and meet all these people looking like this."

He walked over to one of the big closets in the room and opened the door to reveal a ten-foot expanse of bright garments.

"Mrs. Perkins has quite a wardrobe and she seems to have left much of it here. Considering the rent she's charging me, I'm sure she won't mind if we borrow something for a few hours."

Bonita sat down carefully on the edge of the bed, wrapped like some dejected primitive tribeswoman in her striped towel. Her courage in coming here had been dampened along with her clothes. She watched Jordan taking charge of the situation again, and she was in no condition to fight him.

"Oh, there you are," he said to the couple who came in the door. The young man was carrying a large black box labeled MAKEUP and the gray-haired woman was buttoning a smock over her party clothes as she came in.

"Vic Jones and Charlotte Hastings, this is what's left of Bonita Langmeade. You have fifteen minutes to work on her. See if you can find something in this closet that will fit her, put a little makeup on her, she doesn't need much, and see if you can do something about her hair."

They all stood staring at Bonita with equally dubious expressions.

"I have to go back and meet my guests," Jordan said as he headed for the door. "You're in the hands of my best makeup man and my favorite wardrobe lady. If they can't make you look decent, no one can," and with one last chuckle of pleasure at her predicament, he left the room.

She watched him go, feeling mortified at the way he had thrust her into the hands of complete strangers, giving her no opportunity to collect herself and make a protest.

Bonita was dazzled by the professionalism of Jordan's studio employees. While Vic seated her in a chair before the dressing table, Charlotte rifled through the closet quickly. Vic opened his equipment box and spread out an arsenal on the table in front of her.

"I always carry this curling iron for emergencies. You towel your hair dry while I heat it up."

"But I never curl my hair," Bonita said.

"Look, Vic. How about this?" Charlotte said, pulling out a swirl of blue chiffon. "There is no waistline to it so it won't matter if it's too big. It's a one-shouldered number. Can we pile up her hair Grecian style?"

The two ignored her completely as they planned their transformation, and within the time they'd been allotted by their studio boss, she was standing before them for inspection, her dark hair now a mass of curls, caught up loosely with a circlet of silk flowers in various shades of blue and violet that highlighted the dress perfectly.

"I couldn't have picked a better dress for her if I'd had all week," Charlotte mused happily. "Look how much taller it makes her look. And the color sets off her dark hair."

The two seemed not even to consider her a participant in the project and talked over her head as if she were inanimate.

"Don't you like that iridescent pink rouge on her cheeks?" Vic asked proudly. "Brings those cheekbones right up, doesn't it?"

"All right, we're all through," Charlotte said, speaking directly to Bonita for the first time and startling her.

They each stepped to one side of the door like an honor guard, arms extended, as if they expected her to know just how to make a star entrance to the party.

She could almost hear the roll of trumpets as she stepped through the doorway into the crowd of people who were milling through the large rooms of the house. She had never worn chiffon before, and she was surprised at how the dress made her feel. She felt as if she were floating in a cloud, so light were the transparent layers that seemed to lift her feet off the ground.

Each man she passed gave her a look more pleasant and interested than any she'd ever received, and she realized what it felt like to be the glamorous center of attention.

As she entered the living room, everyone turned to look at her and she was flustered by so much attention. She caught sight of Jordan McCaslin guiding some new arrivals toward the bar. He glanced toward her, gave her an appreciative look that opened his face into a vague and automatically friendly smile, then turned back to his guests. Before she had time to realize that his reaction had disappointed her, his head whipped back in her direction, and one eyebrow shot up with a curious bend to it.

"Why, it's you!" he gasped so loudly that she could hear him clearly over the conversations that cut across the room between them.

He came quickly to her side and Bonita was surprised to feel a surge of pleasure under his approving look. She had tried from their first meeting to feel some acceptance from him, and it now seemed ironic that she should get it merely for entering a room. She had never before realized the power a woman can exert by the simple drama of her appearance.

"I didn't recognize you when you came in. They have turned you into quite a stunner!" he said. He placed his hand on her shoulder, left bare by the slant of the neckline, and ran it lightly down her arm to grasp her hand, and then stepped back to inspect her.

She felt a blush creep up her cheeks, making the artfully applied rouge on her face unnecessary.

"And you even wear it with a natural blush. I haven't seen a girl blush in years. Now let me introduce you to some of the important people who are here."

He guided her around the room, and as they passed each conversation group, people stopped talking and stepped back to watch them pass. Bonita recognized some of the Carmel society people she'd only seen in newspaper pictures, and she noticed how they gave her looks of interest just because she was on the arm of the famous producer.

"Here's Dan Evans, the director I told you about. Dan, I'd like you to meet Bonita Langmeade."

Bonita was surprised at the youthful appearance of the man who would be directing the picture. He was dressed more casually than most of the others at the party, and he seemed as nervously out of place as she felt in such stellar company. He took her hand shyly and shook it as if he was the one honored by the introduction.

"I'm so glad to meet you. You've written a beautiful script, just beautiful. I'm looking forward to directing it."

Bonita glanced quickly toward Jordan McCaslin to see if he would add any comment to the young director's praise of the script she'd turned in, but he had set his stark features into a noncommittal smile.

"If you two will excuse me, I see that someone has just arrived," Jordan said, walking away and leaving Bonita to contemplate a conversation with the stranger tensely adjusting his horn-rimmed glasses in front of her. But she need not have worried, for he immediately began gushing his excitement over the project ahead.

"I'm really thrilled to be working with Jordan on

this project. This is my first feature film, and I'm sure I can learn a lot from him. He's already given me interpretations on the script that have been invaluable."

As he continued talking, it became obvious to Bonita why he had been chosen to direct the film, for he was eager to be guided by Jordan McCaslin, and it would be easy for the producer to influence him toward his own opinions.

Dan Evans seemed thrilled by the chance to take Bonita around the room and introduce her to the script girl, the unit manager, and various other people who would be working on the picture, and she glowed under the waves of appreciation that came her way when each person learned who she was. They each eyed her with obviously curious interest, and they had lavish praise for her script. She was surprised to learn that they had all studied every line of it in preparation for whatever duties they had on the picture, but it was impossible to determine from their comments whether the script was still as she had written it, or whether it had been tampered with by Jordan.

Bonita could hear a loud flurry of excitement near the front door, and then she stopped mid-sentence when she recognized the striking redhead who had just made a sweeping entrance into the room, followed by a circle of babbling admirers. It was the famous Kate Harrigan, dressed in a long rustling black taffeta skirt and a low-necked white blouse dripping with lace. The sound of the actress's tinkling laughter filled the suddenly hushed room as everyone stopped what they were doing to take in the surprise of her appearance among them.

With perfect timing her rugged husband appeared just then behind her, creating a second wave of attention from the onlookers. Doug Driver towered over everyone in the room, his tall gaunt frame reminding Bonita instantly of every cowboy, battlefield soldier, or gangster character he had ever portrayed on the screen. His hair was streaked with silver, and his dark eyes blazed with highlights befitting the practised he-man image he had created so successfully during his movie career. His voice boomed across the room with a force that seemed more uncontrolled than one would expect from an actor, but it made the perfect bass accompaniment to the lighter melodies of his wife and acting partner, Kate Harrigan Driver.

They progressed around the room, regally accepting the awed homage of all who came near them, and Bonita wondered as they came closer to her corner of the room what they were doing in Carmel. Perhaps they were personal friends of Jordan, for they were responding to his comments and laughing with him as if they knew him well. Bonita had heard that Doug Driver was an enthusiastic amateur golfer, and she decided they were probably visiting one of the many golf courses in the area and had come to the party to lend some star quality to the proceedings. Before she had time for more speculation, she saw Jordan steering the Drivers straight toward her, and she found herself swept into the charismatic aura of the two superstars who had suddenly aimed their attention in her direction.

"This is Bonita Langmeade, our scriptwriter," Jordan said to the couple, neglecting any further introductions as obviously being unnecessary. For one moment Bonita considered asking to whom she was being introduced, and the ludicrous thought brought a bright mischievous smile to her lips. Since this was very much like being presented to royalty she moved one foot backward and made a deep bow of acknowledgment.

"Charming, what a charming slip of a girl," Doug Driver shouted to everyone in the room.

"Can the script really have been written by such a young child?" Kate Harrigan asked the assemblage, giving Bonita's face an envious inspection and involuntarily reaching toward her own neck and chin as if to check their firmness.

"You've written one hellishly good script, my girl," Doug Driver said to her.

"Oh, you've read it?" she said.

Doug Driver's laughter reverberated through the room, and he was joined by all the bystanders whose merry looks clearly indicated that they thought Bonita had made a terribly clever put-down.

"He read what he could and we helped him with the two-syllable words," Kate Harrigan snapped toward her husband, and he pretended chagrin at her playful insult.

A maid brought a tray of champagne and passed the glasses around, and as the conversation continued, a photographer crouched around the Drivers, snapping candid pictures of them from every angle in constant punctuation to their words. Bonita marveled at their ability to ignore the intrusion, for the noise and distractions in the room were beginning to give her a disoriented feeling. She sipped at her champagne quickly, hoping to ease her dry mouth.

"We think the script is just lovely," Kate was saying to her. "Very unusual and certainly challenging. Especially for Doug. His range has been so limited in the past."

Bonita looked at her blankly, trying to make sense of her words.

"Whose range is limited?" Doug asked. "How about all those barmaid roles you were always playing at Universal?" he chided his wife.

"This picture will be good for both of us. My agent says that being cast in these parts will . . ."

"Being cast in what parts?" Bonita asked, beginning to suspect something she didn't want to believe.

"Why, being cast in your story. Didn't you know? Doug and I are playing the leads in your script."

"Just turn this way, miss. That's it." A flashbulb burst at Bonita from just behind Jordan McCaslin's shoulder, blinding her with its intensity as Kate Harrigan's words made their impact on her simultaneously.

"Oh, you poor dear. You're not used to flashbulbs. Just close your eyes for a moment," Kate said.

Bonita blinked rapidly as bright starburst explosions went off in the dark space around her. She felt someone take the champagne glass from her hand, and she groped for the back of a nearby chair to hold onto. Her vision cleared slowly and the first thing she saw was the face of Jordan McCaslin as he held her glass out to her.

He was watching her attentively, with a calm smile on his lips that left his eyes cold and uninvolved.

"No, just keep it," she stammered at him, noticing that he did not look concerned or seem to fear she would make a scene over the astounding news she'd just heard. He must have known that she could not make any objection right here in front of the actors.

"Excuse me, I'm afraid my eyes are filling with tears," she said, backing away from the group now that she could see more clearly. She turned and bumped into Dan Evans who had been listening at the edges of the conversation.

"Weren't we lucky to get two big stars like the Drivers?" he asked her, but she rushed by him without answering. All her hopes and dreams for the film had been hopelessly smashed with the drastic news that these overly flamboyant actors had been cast to play the sensitive young lovers of her story.

This time, as she passed through the rooms of crowded chattering guests, she took no pleasure from the admiring glances she received. She picked up a floating edge of her chiffon skirt so that she could make her escape more rapidly. It now seemed to her ironic and cruel that Jordan McCaslin would turn her into Cinderella for the party, knowing that she was about to hear some news that would devastate her. No wonder he hadn't wanted her at the party. And once she'd shown up unexpectedly, did he really think he could distract her with the beautiful clothes and the glamorous hairdo so that she would not take notice of the bombshell he was ready to set off beneath her feet? Her eyes were so filled with tears that she almost collided with an overweight guest who was balancing champagne glasses in both of his chubby hands.

"Excuse me," she muttered and with relief found the door to the bedroom and ran inside. She sat on the bed for a few moments and gave in to the tears of rage and frustration that were choking her. Then she realized she would have to change her clothes and leave the party before she had another encounter with Jordan McCaslin. She needed time to think about just how she could fight him on this new dispute.

She went to the bathroom and found that Charlotte had very kindly spread out her clothing in front of a wall heater so that it was now dry though a bit wrinkled. She carefully lifted the blue chiffon cloud over her head and placed it on a hanger, saying good-bye forever to her brief moments of glamor as she did so. She pulled on her warm jeans and had started to button her blouse when she heard a noise in the bedroom. She came out to face Jordan McCaslin.

"Don't you know how to knock?" she snapped at him.

"I had no idea you'd be changing your clothes," he said, watching openly as her fingers did their hasty work at the front of her blouse. "Why aren't you going to stay and enjoy the party? You looked beautiful and this is supposed to be a special day for you," he said, pretending he was unaware of any reason for her unfriendly manner.

"You mean stay out there and smile and chat with

everyone just as if I totally approve of what you're doing to this film? Well, I won't do that. I'm not good at pretending."

"What are you so upset about?"

"What am I upset about? Can you honestly pretend you don't know? I'm upset because you've chosen two middle-aged superstars to play the parts of young, sensitive lovers. Doug and Kate Driver will completely overwhelm the story. They are all wrong for the parts you've cast them in."

Jordan McCaslin sprang across the room toward her with one of his typically energetic moves. She could see his azure eyes flash with bright lightning bolts of anger as he grabbed her shoulders in his strong hands.

"You are a writer, my dear, not a casting director, and your views on the stars of this picture are completely your own and of no concern to me. I think it is time you learned a little bit about this movie business you're now involved in. When a writer sells his story to the movie company, his control over the project ends, and the sooner you learn that the better our working relationship will be. Now, in this case I hired you to write the script, too."

"I suppose you've completely rewritten it by now to suit your own special style."

He gave her an indignant look. "I believe in preserving the integrity of the author's work. I haven't taken out a word of your dialogue. We've had to add some action descriptions, and make some necessary technical changes. That is the producer's responsibility. From now on you'd better understand your role. You are merely an interested observer, available for consultation when it is requested. But if you let your unhappy feelings show, you will ruin the work of this company and I can't allow that."

Bonita pulled herself loose from his grasp and threw herself down at the small chair in front of the dressing table. Her mind swirled with confusion, and she was unable to accept the impact of his words. How could she disengage herself from active involvement in this project? How could she stand by and watch this man tamper with a story he obviously did not understand? In the mirror in front of her she could see Jordan McCaslin fighting to control his anger as he stood behind her. He clenched and unclenched his fists, and when he spoke again, seemed to be making an effort to hold in the angry storm that he had given voice to a moment before.

"All right, Bonita. I don't owe you any explanation, but since it matters so much to you I'll try to explain. One thing that adds great excitement to a film is casting it 'against type.' Do you know what that means?"

She shook her head sadly as with resignation she faced another of his attempts to educate her to his business.

"When you place actors in roles that are completely different from their natural personality types they must work harder to assume their characters and that creates an energy and an excitement in their performances. It will be easy for Kate, she's very anxious to show her more vulnerable and romantic side. And Dan and I have had long talks about Doug. We're going to work with him and tone him down. And he'll give a performance that will make that leading man come alive."

"He'll turn him into a brutal cowboy that she could never fall in love with."

"You are too personally involved with the characters. You just can't see that your story is a handful of starlight, that it needs drama and action."

His criticism, delivered in his usual forceful way, infuriated her.

"All you care about is having box-office stars in the cast so your picture will make a lot of money for your studio," she said, and when she saw in his reflection a look of pain, and knew she had hurt him, she hurried to wound again. "And now you're justifying that decision by pretending it was some sort of artistic choice."

Her insult had affected him, she could tell by his silence.

She reached up to remove the silk cornflowers from her hair so that she could get out of his house as quickly as possible, but the numerous hairpins Vic had used to hold her hair up became tangled as she tried to work too fast. Soon she realized she had made a hopeless mess of it, and the flowers were still fastened in several mysterious ways that she couldn't see. She gave an exasperated sound, and then a startled gasp as she realized that Jordan had come to stand directly behind her and was reaching out to touch her hair.

He was obviously not experienced at such matters, but working from above her head it was easier for him to find the right pins, and in a few moments he had loosened the circlet of flowers and placed it on the table, and then he ran his hands through her hair as he searched for hairpins left behind. She sat meekly cooperative, wondering why it was taking him so long, but pins kept falling, and she kept retrieving them and stacking them neatly before her.

After a few moments she realized he was no longer searching for pins, but his hands were still on her hair, and he was almost stroking her head, smoothing the now jumbled remains of her Grecian curls, trying to lull her with his calming massage. But still he said nothing. Bonita closed her eyes, and leaned back against him, his closeness reminding her of how he had held her in his arms to keep her warm the last time she'd seen him. She marveled at the way he could so skillfully defuse her anger with his touch.

But his damaging words still hung in the room like

icicles that refused to melt in a hot sun. He'd called her story a mere handful of starlight. He considered it flimsy and without substance. He did not know that it was a real story, that everything had happened just as she wrote it, and she swore she would never tell him, for she could already picture what a good laugh that would give him. In his sophisticated world there was no appreciation for the majesty and drama of simply falling in love.

"Are you through? Look at the mess you've made of my hair." She grabbed up a comb and tried to smooth her dark hair, but she was unaccustomed to dealing with curls, and after a few futile attempts she stood up.

"Thanks for letting me join your party, even if I was an uninvited guest."

"I've tried to explain that was an oversight."

"And if you don't mind, I'll leave the way I came in. I don't think I want to face any more of the exuberant enthusiasm of your famous stars out there."

"Bonita . . ." Jordan McCaslin obviously wanted to continue his attempts to mollify her, but before he could say anything more she hurried out the French doors to the patio. She closed them firmly behind her and noticed through the glass that he did not try to follow her but turned slowly back to rejoin his party.

Bonita's steps took her almost automatically across the damp lawn and back to the small tile-roofed gazebo overlooking the sea. She looked down into the surge of the blue-green waters below her and watched the relentless agitation of white froth on the huge rocks that loomed up out of the water. But today the call of the sea birds, the heavy spray of salt in the air, and the drama of the view from Pescadero Point all the way north to the lonely point where the famous Lone Cypress tree clung to nearly bare rock, did not have a calming influence upon her, and she turned and hurried to her car, hoping she could instead still the turmoil in her heart by putting as much distance as possible between herself and Jordan McCaslin.

## CHAPTER FOUR

Just as she had promised, Marlene arrived the next afternoon with a load of dresses over her arm after closing the shop early. She insisted that Bonita try on every garment and followed her to her room to watch and pass judgment. As Bonita slipped in and out of the clothes, Marlene kept up a slow, steady progression of questions, trying to find out what had happened at Jordan McCaslin's party the day before. Bonita was so distracted by hooks and zippers and buttons that she found it difficult to be evasive and told Marlene more details than she intended.

"You just crashed his party, without any invitation? I can't imagine you, of all people, doing such a thing, Bonita. Wasn't he furious with you?"

"He said I was supposed to be invited."

"What else could he say with you standing right there ready to join the party, invited or not?"

"When I went over there I didn't realize the party was going on," Bonita said.

"You're just lucky there were a lot of people there. You'd better not be so pushy with him, dropping in at his house alone and unannounced. He's going to think you're chasing after him. I tried to warn you what he's like with women. I hope you'll give him a cold shoulder from now on."

"Don't worry. Our relationship is so cold you could raise a flock of penguins on it."

Both Bonita and Marlene tipped their heads to one side to study the ensemble Bonita was modeling in front of her mirrored closet door. It was a bright yellow velveteen jumper over a black and white tie-silk blouse, and even Marlene smiled with the realization that it was a stunning complement to Bonita's coloring. Bonita studied her reflection. Her freshly washed hair hung straight, but suddenly she saw it curled among the blue flowers that had decorated it yesterday, and the simple jumper turned into the flowing chiffon she had worn at the party. She remembered how Jordan McCaslin had reacted to the transformation his staff had created, and she remembered that for the first time in her life she had actually felt beautiful. But this was another day, and the queen was now a mere commoner. She quickly slipped out of the dress and blouse.

"As I've told you already, Marlene, I don't want any more clothes. Even this pretty one doesn't tempt me. I'm sorry you went to so much trouble for me."

"Oh, it's no trouble," Marlene said, sitting down to watch Bonita put the dresses back on their hangers. "Now tell me who was at the party."

Alberta Langmeade's voice called up the stairs. "Bonita, there's a telephone call for you. Take it on the hall phone, will you, dear?"

"Who is it, Grandmother?" Bonita called down the stairs as she stepped out into the hall in her slip.

"He didn't say."

Bonita had only to hear a few syllables over the telephone line before she recognized the familiar strident tones of Doug Driver.

"Little lady, I'm sorry you left that party last night so early. Kate and I were just sitting here sipping our scotch and saying how we would love to get to know you better, so she made me pick up the phone and give you a call. Why don't you come on over and have dinner with us tonight?"

"Dinner, tonight?"

"We're staying right here in the valley at the Quail Lodge. Jordan told me we're not far down the road from your place. So you hurry on over here and the three of us will chow down together, what do you say?"

"Well, I don't know."

"Kate doesn't take no for an answer, so you'd better be careful what you say."

Bonita was dismayed at first by the idea of spending an evening with the overpowering Mr. and Mrs. Driver. Then it occurred to her that perhaps this was just the solution to her problem that she had been looking for. Jordan McCaslin had made it clear that he was not interested in her opinions on the project, but the Drivers might be more receptive to her suggestions. And she was sure that she wouldn't have any trouble conversing with the famous couple. From what she had observed at the party they kept up a pretty constant patter all by themselves.

"I am very flattered by your invitation," she said, stating her feelings very frankly.

"We're in a cottage right by the golf course, so you just come on over and we'll have a few belts and then wander over to The Covey when we get hungry, okay?" Obviously Doug Driver did not expect to be turned down, for he rang off the line before Bonita had a chance to say another word.

When Bonita turned around she saw Marlene standing in the bedroom doorway, unashamed of her obvious eavesdropping.

"I guess I'll need that yellow outfit after all," Bonita said.

"Sounds like you have a big date tonight."

"Yes, if you'll excuse me I have to hurry and get ready."

"He doesn't give you much notice, does he?"

"What? Oh, well I guess they just thought of it. It's a kind of a spur of the moment idea."

"They? Oh, come on Bonita, stop being so mysterious. It doesn't suit you."

"All right, Marlene. That was Doug Driver. He and his wife want me to come over to the Quail Lodge where they are staying and have dinner at The Covey."

"Kate Harrigan and Doug Driver have invited *you* to have dinner with them? But *why?*"

"They are going to be the stars of the picture and I guess they want to talk about the script."

In order to hurry Marlene on her way, Bonita slipped into a robe and helped her carry the rest of the dresses downstairs. Marlene stalled and asked questions all the way, unable to believe that her friend had been granted a private audience with such important people.

As Bonita took her bath and dressed she began to wonder if she was equipped to hand out advice to the Drivers on how they should approach their difficult new roles. But realizing that they had made the first move, insisting she come and get to know them, she decided she would let them take the lead, and if they asked her opinion she would give it. This was perhaps the perfect opportunity to make her influence felt on the picture. Meeting with the actors privately, without Jordan McCaslin knowing about it, might be the way to save the project, and that thought made her approach the evening with more courage.

The Drivers had taken over one of the hotel's cottage suites, a circle of four bedrooms around a large living room furnished in bright-colored contemporary bamboo furniture with a large plate-glass window that looked out onto the golf course where golfers whirred by in their electric carts from time to time as they hurried to finish their rounds before dark. When Bonita entered the room she was surprised to see various members of the Driver entourage milling about. There was a secretary, and an older married couple who apparently served as combination hairdressers, confidants, or golf partners as needed. But Kate Harrigan quickly shooed them out of the room and settled beside the modern fireplace with its gas-flamed ceramic log to give Bonita her undivided attention.

"Doug will join us in a minute. He's taking a shower. You know, he thinks he's in heaven with three golf courses right here in the valley, and all those Pebble Beach courses as well. Every day that we aren't shooting I'll know where to find him, chasing that ridiculous white ball around with a stick."

Bonita was surprised to see that Kate Harrigan, wearing only a minimum of makeup, looked younger and more beautiful than when she'd seen her last night under a thick layer of beauty aids. Her skin had a luminous quality, and her eyes, now out from under their overpowering green eye shadow tenting, sparkled with color of their own.

"I hope you know how excited Doug and I are about making this picture. Doug has worked with Jordan McCaslin before, but this is my first picture for him."

"Does Doug find him easy to work with?"

"Doug finds everyone easy to work with. But frankly, I'm a bit frightened of Jordan, aren't you?" Kate leaned forward conspiratorially. "He is a very opinionated fellow, and he won't accept any compromise when it comes to his work. I just hope I can give a performance that will please him. I always worry about whether I can live up to my publicity."

Bonita was surprised to see a hint of insecurity in Kate Harrigan's unexpectedly hesitant words. She couldn't imagine that this experienced actress could share her own feelings of awe when confronted by the aloof persistence of Jordan McCaslin.

"He is just a bit . . . overpowering . . . isn't he?" Bonita asked cautiously.

"Well, you know the story behind his mournful face, don't you? Maybe not, it is one of those less-known Hollywood legends."

Kate drew her chair closer to Bonita's as if they were in danger of being overheard in this private sitting room. "You see, Jordan was once in love with an actress. I won't say her name. Well, why not? He was in love with Kit Lawrence. She was working at the same studio I was. In fact, she got that part in *Loveless* because I was on suspension, and that's the part that made her a star overnight. Well, anyway . . ."

"Hollywood gossip!" Doug Driver called out from the doorway of his bedroom. He was dressed for dinner, but still had a towel around his shoulders and his hair was tousled into a ruffled nest of black and silver. Bonita wasn't sure, but she thought the nest looked considerably more sparse than usual.

"Can't you talk about anything else, woman? You scream at all the columnists and fan magazines, but you do a better job of spreading stories than they will ever do."

"Oh, be quiet and go hide yourself until you get your toupee on. Do you want to frighten this poor child to death? She's never seen a balding cowboy before."

"I'm looking for Mike to help me with it."

"All I'm doing is trying to explain to Bonita the tragic love story in Jordan McCaslin's past that's made him into such an ogre."

One of the Drivers' aides came scurrying to join Doug in his room after being summoned with several loud shouts from the thinly thatched he-man.

"Close the door, Mike. I've heard this story before," Doug called loudly enough for Kate to hear, and before the door closed Kate had time for her parting shot to him.

"If you hadn't heard it you'd be right here lapping it up. You're the Male Gossip of the Year winner every time."

Bonita couldn't wait for Kate to get on with her story. She was tantalized to think that she might finally learn the secret of Jordan McCaslin's life. Perhaps knowing the truth about him would help her to understand the odd barrier that seemed to exist between them, quite apart from their professional quarrel. At times she sensed that he was trying to draw close to her, establish some sort of personal rapport. But just when he had lulled her into that warm encirclement, he'd pull back cruelly, leaving her unsure of her relationship with him and suspicious of his motives.

"Now, where was I? Oh, yes. Kit Lawrence. Well, she wasn't the Kit Lawrence you see on the silver screen today. She was a struggling young starlet from nowheresville, and I guess Jordan just fell for her fluttering false eyelashes and her baby lisp in spite of himself. You must remember he was much younger then, too. I don't think he'd give such a ninny a second look today. Oh, excuse me, I haven't offered you a drink. The bar's right over there."

"No, thank you. Go on with your story."

"Well, Jordan coached her, he introduced her to people, he taught her how to dress and conduct herself in public, and God knows she needed all the help she could get. And I guess he thought they were lifetime co-stars. But as soon as she signed that five-picture contract and started making it big, she dropped him like a hot potato. She found herself bigger game —oilmen and princes and gorgeous musclemen—and she wouldn't let her answering service even put through Jordan's calls."

The story was a familiar one. It had happened to countless people in Hollywood as well as in every other business where the stakes are high and the participants highly motivated. But this particular story evoked an unexpectedly strong surge of sympathy in Bonita. She could picture those cerulean eyes of Jordan's dimmed with disillusionment and pain. She could imagine how used and ineffectual he must have felt. The ambitious young actress had drained him of all his youthful vitality and he'd replaced it with the empty nervous energy of work that now animated him.

Kate Harrigan was building to the big finish of her story. She lowered her voice as if she were reciting Ophelia's mad scene, placed both of her expressive hands across her breasts, approximately over her heart, looked away from Bonita as if she could not bear to share these terrible words with another mortal, and said slowly, "He resolved never to love again."

Bonita was not sure whether it was Kate's spirited rendition of the story or the story itself that had moved her, but she sat silently studying the fire and saying nothing for several moments. Kate sat back on her chair with the pleased look of someone who had given another talented performance, apparently drawing as much satisfaction from the sight of Bonita's pale face and trembling lips as from a standing ovation in a theater. She looked quite irritated when her husband came into the room and broke the mood.

"Get your jewels on, Mama, we're going to meet our public."

Kate Harrigan rose with a sigh and went to a large jewelry box on a table nearby. She unlocked it and withdrew three fabulous pieces made of turquoise and diamonds. The simple blue dress she'd been wearing was suddenly transformed by the addition of the necklace and bracelets, and she instantly took on her familiar look of a movie queen.

As they strolled toward the restaurant, crossing an arched wooden bridge over the beautifully landscaped man-made lake, Doug Driver chatted with Bonita as familiarly as if they had known each other all their lives, and traded barbs with his wife unceasingly.

"I'm glad Kate told you that story, even if she did ham it up unmercifully.

"If you had told it, we'd still be on verses one through three," Kate snapped.

"No, seriously," Doug said, "I know Jordan Mc-Caslin better than you two. Sometimes he's moody and sometimes he's so bull-headed you want to take him out and thrash him, but you've got to remember that for him his work is everything. His pictures are his lovers now."

As they entered the restaurant, the maitre d' recognized the Drivers at once and hurried to ready a center table by the window overlooking the lake, where all his patrons could get a clear view of the famous guests. Kate posed with a lifted chin and an unnatural smile and accepted the open stares of everyone in the room for a moment, and then before they were shown to their table put her arm around Bonita and drew her close to whisper in her ear, "I'm glad we have you on this picture. I think you can be a softening influence on Jordan. Maybe your love story will convince him that there is still romance in the world." She gave Bonita a secret wink before she began her regal walk through the room toward their table.

Kate's words reassured Bonita, for she felt now that the Drivers did understand that this picture was different from Jordan's usual gutsy epics, and that they would try, within their capabilities, to remain true to the original intent of the story.

Doug was careful to take the menu, and therefore any temptation to order the thick soup or the breaded abalone, away from his dieting wife. He ordered a Covey's Nest of shrimp in a tomato (with *no* dressing on it, he commanded the waiter) and some simple broiled filet of sole for his wife, and she suffered the thorn of her profession with good humor.

"I've got fifteen pounds to lose before we begin filming next week," she confided to Bonita. "I had Charlotte fit my costumes good and tight so that I'd have to lose them. Take off fifteen pounds and you take off fifteen years, my agent says."

"But look out the day the picture's done," Doug laughed, pouring them all some white wine. "She'll gain it all back so fast that if you're standing too close to her you're liable to get yourself knocked over."

Bonita enjoyed the high-calorie meal that Doug had ordered for her and for himself, and the surprisingly easy conversation that the three of them shared as they enjoyed the view of a flock of floating ducks on the lake just outside the window.

Bonita explained to them that the grounds of the Quail Lodge had been declared a wildlife refuge and that the ten lakes that had been built into the golf course design now harbored a large population of birds. They seemed sincerely interested and urged her to introduce them to a waiter she spotted across the room who was a school friend of hers.

Danny came over and told them that the staff members at the Lodge were so intent on protecting the bird population that from March through June, during duck laying season, they all took nets and scooped the bird eggs from the lakes, taking them home to incubate them, safe from the possums, badgers, raccoons, and housecats that might otherwise destroy them. Danny had several ducklings at home now and he promised Kate that he'd bring them to her suite to show them to her when he was ready to return them to the lake.

Not until they had finished dinner and were enjoying their coffee and brandy and the twinkling reflection of lights on the dark water outside did Bonita venture into the topic of the movie they were about to begin work on. Kate was explaining to her the makeup and costume tests they'd already filmed in Hollywood and Bonita suddenly felt bold enough to say, "I would love to see you play this part with very little makeup on. The girl you're playing would never have worn mascara or eye shadow. And I think your face is so expressive just the way it is tonight, natural."

"But my eyeliner, my nose lightener. I've never worked without those," Kate said, suddenly girlish in her uncertainty.

"They must make you feel like you're talking through a mask. You probably have to work much harder to convey your real personality when your face is so camouflaged," Bonita said.

"Why, Bonita, you have a real feel for understanding the actor's problems," Kate said. "I think you've made a good point. I'm going to talk to Vic about it."

"Now don't do anything rash and drop your love-goddess image, Kate, my dear," Doug laughed heartily. "That would mean you'd never get to do another of those laced-up-bodice costume pics you love so much."

At that moment Bonita was startled to see a familiar face across the room. Marlene Webb had just entered the dining room and was carefully searching the room with her languid eyes. As Bonita watched her curiously, she saw a tall man step out of the shadows behind Marlene to grasp her elbow. The two must have heard Doug's laughter ring out across the room, for they immediately started down the steps and toward the table.

"Why it's Jordan McCaslin," Kate said from her viewpoint facing the approaching couple.

"And look at that pretty package he's found to escort," Doug said, standing up to greet them. "Fancy meeting you here. Come and join us," he called in a voice so hearty that Bonita was afraid every person in the room would accept the invitation.

Jordan's eyes met Bonita's for just an instant as he introduced Marlene to the Drivers, and their accusatory glint told Bonita at once that he was not happy to have found her with the Drivers. She wondered how he had the uncanny ability to put her on the defensive with one look when it was she who should be angry for having him barge in on her private evening.

Doug drew up extra chairs and ordered a round of drinks. Marlene slithered into place between the two men. She could no doubt read the shock and surprise in Bonita's face at seeing her with Jordan, and she stared back across the table at Bonita, obviously enjoying her moment of triumph. Then she leaned toward Doug and with her most breathlessly belabored speaking style said, "I was so disappointed to have missed meeting you at the big welcoming party at Jordan's house yesterday that I called him to see if my invitation had been lost like Bonita's."

"Accidents do happen," Jordan interjected with a twisted grin in Bonita's direction.

"And he said he'd try to make it up to me by introducing me to you tonight, since I knew you were here with Bonita. You see, I am an actress myself, and it is a great thrill for me to meet two such honored members of my profession."

Marlene went on and on with her obsequious homage while Doug and Kate accepted it with bored looks of resignation that indicated they were very used to it, but still not comfortable in reacting with the obligatory modesty.

Bonita sat back in her chair and glared at Jordan. How thrilled he must have been by Marlene's brash telephone call and the information she so innocently provided him. He was looking very pleased with himself, for he had found out about her meeting with the Drivers and at the same time found with Marlene the perfect excuse to interrupt it.

When Kate was able to disentagle herself from

Marlene's barrage of compliments, she turned to Jordan with a flair of excitement in her eyes again. "Bonita has come up with the most wonderful idea for me. She thinks I should play this picture with a whole new makeup look. You know, Vic and I weren't really happy with those tests, and . . ."

"I wasn't aware that Bonita was a makeup expert," Jordan said, his voice giving warning that storm clouds were gathering over the table.

"I don't think Bonita knows a powder puff from a rouge pot," Marlene said.

"Well, she knows the characters she's created," Kate said, "and as she said . . ."

"I gather she's said quite a bit this evening," Jordan interrupted his star. "Now may a qualified expert say something? What is important is that my female lead appear young. This is a story of young love, as Bonita has taken such pains to remind me so often. And I think that as we do more tests, Vic and I will be able to make the proper decision concerning the makeup without Bonita's interference."

Kate gave Bonita one of her famous expressive looks that was worth pages of dialogue. She seemed to be telling Bonita, "We were right. He is impossible. But I can be impossible, too!" She was not a woman who had to give in at the first sign of opposition, and she tossed her mane of red hair as she prepared to stand up to the stubborn producer.

"You want *young*? I'll give you young. But as an actress I'll tell you this: The best way to portray youth is with a look of naturalness and innocence. Not more and more makeup."

Bonita was proud of Kate's determined stance, especially since Kate had let her glimpse her vulnerable side and Bonita knew that the actress felt some uncertainty about working with Jordan McCaslin. She decided she had to back her up.

"I think Kate has a good grasp of the character.

I think with her awareness of the sensitive nature of the girl, no matter how she's made up she can convey . . ."

Bonita stopped speaking mid-sentence, for Jordan McCaslin was signaling with every muscle of his body that he would listen to no more. He straightened from a slightly slouched position in his chair, put his brandy snifter down, and stared at her with widened eyes that telegraphed their malevolence. Everyone at the table tensed in preparation for the attack that was coming. And when it came, it was more powerful for the control he seemed to be exerting over himself. He did not raise his voice. Neither did he pound the table or unleash a terrible torrent of words. He said with a frosty calmness that belied the fire in his eyes, "Being a newcomer to the picture business, Bonita, you are obviously not aware of how unethical it is for you to meet privately with the actors and try to influence their performances. We have a director for that, and as the producer I will supervise his interpretations. You must not interfere any further with the actors or I'll have you barred from the set."

Everyone at the table was aware that Jordan had fired the fatal shot, and to cover their embarrassment they all erupted into a flurry of small talk. Bonita tried to be gracious and appear unhurt by his attack so that the others wouldn't feel uncomfortable. But as Marlene entertained them with Carmel gossip, and Doug Driver gave a rumbling account of the wildlife he had encountered at the water hazards on the golf course that afternoon, Bonita's mind tumbled over and over itself as outrage chased frustration. Jordan McCaslin was sure that his public chastisement would silence her comments on the picture forever, but she would find a way to get around him. Perhaps Doug and Kate would remain her allies, in spite of their producer's warnings. Or maybe the young director would listen to her.

The most obvious technique would be to continue her efforts to influence Jordan McCaslin, but in a more devious way. If she were to appear cooperative, perhaps he would let her remain an observer. And maybe by avoiding all these direct confrontations she could subtly make him hear her voice. But then she looked at Jordan across the table, with the cruel set of his determined jaw and the cynical smile that burned so shallowly, and realized that she could never pretend an alliance with this man. Jordan McCaslin was not a man to be toyed with.

The women in the group began discussing topics that interested them, and the men had withdrawn into their own private conversation. Bonita listened half-heartedly as Marlene laboriously explained to Kate her opinions on the latest fashions in clothing. While pretending interest in one conversation, she couldn't help leaning in her chair slightly to listen in on the other.

Jordan was telling Doug Driver, "You see, I want my story to have tension to it all the way through. I want my heroine to convey her resistance so that my hero will try every means he can to get through her wall of shyness. You know what I mean. Remember . . ."

Jordan talked on quietly to Doug, obsessed as usual with the project he was working on. *My* story, *my* hero, *my* heroine, he was saying. He was talking as if he were the mastermind behind the entire project, as if the scenario belonged to him alone. She felt as jealous as a young mother watching someone else take her child to his first circus. It was her story and she wanted to be the one to enjoy it, to nourish it, and to be responsible for its growth and development. She was the only one who could do it right.

Doug Driver had an early morning tee-off time and called a halt to the party rather early, much to Bonita's relief. As they walked through the high-ceilinged glass lobby of the hotel toward the front entrance, Marlene clung to Jordan's arm, and Kate and Doug walked together, their arms around each other's waist but chirping insults to each other.

Bonita walked behind the foursome alone, but did not feel like a fifth wheel until Marlene asked her as they stepped outside, "Where's Brad tonight?"

And then without waiting for an answer, Marlene said to Jordan as he helped her into his limousine, "It's such a shame Brad couldn't be here with her tonight to make the party complete."

## CHAPTER FIVE

During the following week spring rains dampened the valley almost every day, giving the fields of lacy artichoke plants and the geometrically planted orchards an earthy odor of fertility, and the surrounding Santa Lucia mountains a misted ethereal look. The rain gave Bonita just the excuse she needed to stay inside the house and avoid the organized chaos that was erupting all over her grandmother's ranch, transforming the formerly idyllic hideaway into something like a downtown intersection. Even Alberta seemed dismayed by the number of people who had descended on her property.

One entire pasture had been converted into a parking lot and several semi-trucks full of props, costumes, and photographic equipment were parked there. The parking circle was lined with mobile homes which were being stored until they were to be used as star dressing rooms, offices, and portable commissaries during the filming at Brad's ranch and elsewhere on location.

Out in the barn a busy crew had installed film editing benches and racks on which to store the large 35-millimeter film cans, and the loft had been converted into a screening area with projectors and folding chairs, so that the cast and staff could view the daily film as it was returned from the processing lab. In one corner of the barn camera and lighting equipment had been set up so that various tests could be filmed against a plain muslin backdrop.

Brad came over almost daily to report to Bonita and her grandmother on the bizarre changes that were taking place at his ranch.

"They're painting my house. They had so many painters they did the whole house on Monday before it rained. You won't believe this, but they're painting it *old!* I mean, first they painted it yellow because this McCaslin fellow insisted it had to be a yellow ranch house. Now they're going over the paint and sponging on some dirty stuff so it won't look freshly painted. Can you believe that?"

Bonita remembered that in her original magazine story she had fleetingly described the house the girl lived in as being yellow, but later when writing the script she had left out that incidental detail. She was amazed that Jordan had gone back to the original material and insisted on such strict adherence to fact.

The next day Brad brought some more news. "They moved my olive tree! Just dug a huge hole around it and moved it. McCaslin looked through that little black thing he carries around and said the tree was blocking his view of the hills in the background, so the next day when I came out the thing was sitting twenty yards down the front walk. I tell you, Bonita, these movie people are crazy."

The night before filming was to start Brad came over to sit on the front porch with Bonita and watch the flurry of movie people up and down her driveway.

"Now they've offered to make actors out of my horses," he said. "They'll pay me a fee for every one of them they use in the picture. Can you imagine?"

"I'm sorry I dragged you into this, Brad," Bonita said.

"Aw, I don't mind. Look at all the dough I'm making for just sitting back and watching. I'll be able to buy those new mares I've been wanting."

"But don't you mind having all those people around?"

"They're not so bad. They've got a stuntwoman with them that really knows her horses. I've been taking her out riding every day so she can decide which horses to use. And the guys working around there are real nice. They kind of tease me about things, but ...."

Bonita looked at him questioningly but he did not finish the thought. He seemed suddenly embarrassed and changed the subject.

"When they're all gone I'll appreciate the peace and quiet we've got here more than ever."

"And you'll have a fresh coat of dirty yellow paint on your house, too," she laughed.

"I just hope that you'll get all this moviemaking out of your system and we can get back to normal around here in a hurry," Brad said.

He put his arm around her shoulders in a more possessive way than he had ever touched her. "You and I have a future to talk about as soon as we're rid of this crazy present we're living with."

She looked at him for a long moment, wondering why he was suddenly making such a forced attempt to change the carefree relationship that she had always enjoyed with him. He had never made any demands of her, never tried to discuss anything personal with her before, and she had appreciated that and been able to maintain a close friendship with him because of it. Perhaps he could now feel outside forces pulling her away from him, and away from the simple life they both shared. And perhaps that had aroused feelings of competition in him.

She stood up, wondering if he was now hoping for more of a commitment from her, a sign that she felt something for him which would keep her bound to him here forever. She hurried to change the subject, unsure of how she wanted to respond.

"Looks like the weather will be clear for the filming tomorrow morning. They are lucky."

"That art director fellow said they won't be using my place until next week. Where are they going to be tomorrow?" Brad asked her.

"Well, Mr. McCaslin was kind enough to send me a shooting schedule. Through the United States Mail, I might add. It says they're going to be filming on the Seventeen-Mile Drive, right at the Spanish Bay, I think. It's a beach scene in the early part of the story when the young lovers first meet. Do you want to come and watch?"

"That might be kind of interesting. What time shall I pick you up?"

"You'll have to be here no later than six because they start shooting promptly at seven o'clock in the morning. They need to get as much done as possible before the afternoon sun moves into view over the ocean. That was explained to me by my grandmother who is now a cinematic expert."

They both laughed together, relaxed again like old friends, as Brad walked toward his pickup truck.

Bonita stood on a windy cliff above South Moss Beach the next morning, pulling her wraparound coat tightly around her. She felt sorry for Kate and Doug who were rehearsing a scene on the beach below in skimpy summer clothing. They had to pretend it was a hot sunny day, perfect for strolling on the beach, while Bonita's teeth were chattering with the early morning cold. Bonita laughed as she saw Kate lift up her ankle-length skirt and petticoat to show some bystanders her long red underwear beneath.

Bonita and Brad were standing together, observing the movie company from afar, but several people recognized Bonita and waved to her to come on down and watch from the sand so that she could hear what was going on. As they worked their way down to the beach, Bonita looked at the beautiful bay Jordan McCaslin had chosen as the location for this important scene in the picture. With the cooperation of the local authorities, Jordan's men had removed every nearby picnic bench and covered all the paved roads in the area with a layer of sand. They had also cleverly disguised the railings at the cliff edges and the coin-operated telescopes used by the tourists for observing the sea lions on the offshore rocks by fastening enough branches to them so they resembled native shrubbery.

This was the way Bonita liked this bay. Facing the sea, with the camera equipment and movie trailers behind her, she could imagine she was seeing this historic bit of coastline just as Don Gaspar de Portola had when he camped here in 1769 on his expedition from Baja California. Portola had been trying to locate Monterey Bay, and discouraged by his failure, he decided on this spot to make the arduous trip back to San Diego. It wasn't until his second expedition that he progressed to the true Monterey Bay, just around the next bend in the coastline.

She looked toward the sharp rise of land jutting into the water to her left, forming the southern rim of the bay. Early mariners had often mistaken Point Joe for the entrance to Monterey Bay and become shipwrecked on the dangerous rocks. Bonita knew that the

*Celia,* the *Flavel* and the *Roderick Dhu* had all gone down right in these turbulent waters.

As Bonita and Brad finally reached the beach and joined the milling crowd of moviemakers, Bonita was saddened to think about the rumors she'd heard that a hotel was going to be built on this bay, with yet another golf course nearby. She felt strongly that this coastline was meant to be savored in solitary privacy, not from the confines of a crowd.

"Quiet on the set, please. This is a rehearsal," a young voice called out and suddenly the beach was as still of human voices as if Doug and Kate were all alone. She could not hear what they were saying because they were speaking softly beneath a microphone that a boom man was dangling over their heads on a long pole. Kate's red hair was billowing romantically in the sea breezes, and her face, while covered with a considerable amount of pancake makeup, looked as if it would photograph quite naturally, and Bonita was pleased with the youthfulness Kate seemed to be projecting.

"All right, that's enough," called a familiarly commanding voice from a cluster of technicians nearby. Jordan McCaslin removed some headphones he'd been wearing and strode over to where Dan Evans was crouched near the actors. The entire assembly waited expectantly to hear what the producer had to say.

"Let's kill that microphone, Dan. We're picking up too much surf noise. We'll have to dub in the voices later with a wild track."

"Right, Jordan," Dan said, jumping to his feet to make the arrangements.

During the moments of activity that followed, Bonita watched Jordan stride off toward the large camera crane that had been installed on the beach. He sat down on the small perch behind the camera usually occupied by the cinematographer, and gave a signal to the crane operator. The camera and his seat behind it suddenly rose upward without a sound until he was about twenty feet in the air. He studied the scene below him, first through the camera lens and then leaning around the camera to watch the couple who were now standing in the exact positions where Kate and Doug had just been. Doug was now busy on the sidelines having his windblown "hair" rearranged and Kate was discussing some wardrobe problem with Charlotte.

"Stand-ins," Jordan called. "Take the original positions for a walk-through."

Looking upward, Bonita could see that the puffy white clouds that always followed a sequence of spring showers were dabbed across the sky, and Jordan McCaslin seemed to be suspended among them, making decisions and giving directions with the omnipotence of a supreme authority. Bonita had to smile to herself at the perfect picture he made. If only he could grasp two lightning bolts in his hands like Jupiter, he'd be perfectly happy in his godlike pose. When she heard him thunder out another order to someone on the ground, she turned to Brad and sarcastically mumbled, "Yes, lord," and Brad let out a guffaw of pleasure.

Bonita saw Jordan look down at the people beneath him, concentrating so intently that his face seemed to be carved in the white marble of the busts of Roman emperors. He must have heard the sound of Brad's laugh, for as soon as he spotted him, a look of annoyance disturbed his immobile features and he made an imperious gesture that indicated he wished to be lowered to earth. He spoke to one of his young assistants and in just a moment the young man came over to speak to Brad.

"I'm sorry, sir, but this is a closed set and all visitors will have to leave."

Bonita gasped with shock, and decided that for once in her life she would try to exert some influence.

"I happen to be the writer of the script, and Mr. Stark is my guest."

"I know Brad, I've been over at his place working all week. And I know he's a special friend of yours," the young man smiled at her as if he knew more about them than there was to know. "But rules are rules, and a closed set means no visitors. Mr. McCaslin feels that having extra people around makes the cast nervous."

Bonita took a quick look around at the forty or fifty people crowded behind the cameras and wondered whether the addition of one more person made the difference, or whether Jordan McCaslin had objected to this one person because it was Brad Stark. Jordan had treated Brad with open hostility from the moment he'd met him, and Bonita could not see any reason for it. Jordan was not known for his charm or politeness, but why was he going out of his way to single out Brad for such special rudeness? Brad accepted the ruling with equanimity, for the slow pace of filmmaking obviously held no fascination for him.

"I'm going. I've got other things I should be doing, anyway. I'm sure you can hitch a ride back with someone."

"No, wait. You just stay here. I'm not going to let Jordan McCaslin send us instructions by way of one of his flunkies." Bonita started to march indignantly in the direction of Jordan McCaslin, but Brad grabbed her arm with a strong hand and stopped her.

"Now don't get your feathers all ruffled. Look, the man doesn't like me and he's the boss here, so let's not make a big thing of it. They'll be out at the ranch all next week and he can't send me off my own property, so I'll get to watch this gang of gypsies at work all I want."

He pulled her closer to him with a crudely affectionate gesture that took Bonita by surprise, and she lost her footing in the sand where she was standing and fell against his broad chest. Rather than helping her to stand straight, Brad clutched her to him with a smothering armlock.

"Calm down, little dove," he said.

"All right, but that man's attitude makes me mad." She pushed herself out of Brad's arms, clumsily trying to regain her balance on the loose sand, and wondering how to handle Brad's changed manner toward her.

When Brad finally walked away, Bonita could see that Jordan McCaslin was standing facing her directly. He had been watching them from behind Brad, and still had a glowering look on his face. Before he could make whatever unpleasant comment was on his mind, Dan Evans approached him for some consultation. After their quick conference Jordan walked away without another look in her direction.

Dan Evans came over to Bonita, and as he chatted with her the young director bounced first on one leg and then the other, stopping only now and then to nervously adjust his glasses as they slid down his narrow nose. The day was no longer so cold that his constant movement could be explained as keeping him warm. Bonita decided he was keyed up by his anxiety over pleasing his producer.

"How are things going?" she ventured.

"Slowly, very slowly," he said. "But that's typical the first day."

"Well, if I can be of any help," she said, "just let me know. I mean, if you want to talk over any script points or anything, that's why I'm here."

Dan shot a quick glance in the direction Jordan had taken, then lowered his voice for complete privacy.

"Oh, gee, I'm not used to that. See, on the television shows I've directed I've never even met the writers. And besides, Jordan will be going over the script pages with me every night before we shoot them, and he's told me not to discuss them with anyone else."

"Dan Evans, we're ready for a take," Jordan's voice summoned him over a loudspeaker.

"But thanks anyway, Bonita. That's awfully nice of you."

*So much for influencing the director,* Bonita thought.

As the morning progressed, the film progressed by mere inches. It seemed to Bonita that most of the time was spent waiting. The stand-ins played gin rummy, Kate worked on some needlepoint, and Doug swung a golf club back and forth for practice as they all killed time during the long technical breaks between the short takes. Of all the people on the beach, only Jordan McCaslin seemed constantly busy, buoying up the entire company with the energy of his restless movement, always talking to someone on his staff or watching intently as Dan Evans conducted the rehearsals and filming.

Bonita at first hung back on the edge of the crowd of onlookers, but gradually she worked her way forward whenever she was sure she could move closer without interfering with someone's work or line of sight. Soon she was crouched on the sand close to the action, right beside the folding canvas chair that had been set up for the script girl, and she looked over her shoulder to study the pages the girl was marking with numbers and notes. The dialogue on the pages they were currently shooting seemed to be faithful to the words Bonita had submitted, but the screenplay had been printed up with many additional descriptions of action just as Jordan had told her.

"All right, quiet everybody. Stand by. This will be a take," a voice called out for the twentieth time that morning.

The script girl next to Bonita suddenly tensed, scanned her notes, then stopped everyone to call out some important information.

"His left hand should be in his pocket."

"Thanks, honey," Doug rumbled, and quickly moved

so that his stance would exactly match the shot just preceding this one which had been filmed over an hour ago.

Doug looked younger than usual today, and finally Bonita realized as she watched him that it was because the silver glimmers in his hair had disappeared. His hair, both what he grew himself and what he bought and fastened on, was now uniformly dark brown. The dye job was done so well that the new hair color made his skin look tanner and healthier than ever.

"All right, stand by *again*, folks. This is really a take," the tired voice on the microphone announced. "Speed. Action!"

By now the young lovers in the story had met each other for the first time. They had walked together, and talked, and planned when they would meet again. They were about to part, and Kate Harrigan was looking suitably winsome and flirtatious. But Bonita was giving most of her attention to Doug, for she was concerned over his performance. He seemed to be blustering and bullying in his typically heavyhanded acting style.

Suddenly Bonita drew in her breath as if she had been slapped. Kate had playfully started to walk away from him and Doug had grabbed her so roughly that she fell to the sand. He lunged toward her again, and in the ensuing tussle in the sand he savagely grabbed her hands and held them behind her back and then kissed her again and again.

Bonita looked around to see when the cameras would be turned off, but the cameraman on the crane began a silent ascent until he was floating above the couple, then pulled back from them so that much of the beautiful beach would be in his frame. Bonita waited for someone to stop this mistake, but everyone was silent, motionless, letting Doug continue to force himself on the young girl struggling in the sand beneath him. Finally the girl rolled out from under him and Bonita was amazed to see her laughing as the cameras rolled on. Then Doug kissed her one last time, and during this kiss her arms went willingly around his neck.

There was a moment more of silence while Bonita waited for someone to call out for retakes. Obviously Kate and Doug were playing some sort of trick on everyone. But Dan Evans's excited voice called out, "Cut. Print it! Great job, everyone. That was our dinner shot, let's break for lunch."

Immediately an electric excitement took over the crowd as everyone began talking and moving at once, happy to have contributed in some way to making the scene go so well, and now anxious to shut things down and take the reward, a box lunch from the commissary truck.

Bonita turned to the script girl beside her. "Is that the way they rehearsed it?"

"Yes, wasn't it wonderful? Those two make quite a team! Imagine getting it just right in one take."

Bonita saw Jordan McCaslin slap Dan Evans on the shoulder approvingly, which must have given Dan such a happy appetite that he was actually whistling as he hurried toward the lunch tables. Jordan climbed the cliff behind him, but headed toward one of the trailers parked in a row out of camera range. Bonita took special note of which trailer he'd gone into and started to follow him, but then instead stayed with the rest of the crowd as they quickly deserted the beach and headed for lunch.

Next to the commissary truck someone had set up big white tables and spread them with bright blue tablecloths that were flapping in the breeze. The atmosphere indeed resembled a gypsy camp. A man leaned out the window of the truck to pass a white box to each member of the crew. Bonita stood dumbly watching everyone, feeling racked by her indecision.

"Come on and join us, dear," Charlotte said as she

and Vic made a place for Bonita at their table. Bonita took off her coat and laid it on the folding chair they'd offered her, for it was now quite sunny and warm despite the offshore breeze. Then she stood again for a long time, not moving, trying to compose herself and decide what to do next. She had never before felt so stymied and unsure of herself.

"Go get your lunch, dear, right over there. The chicken is delicious," Charlotte said, noticing Bonita's odd mood. "Didn't the morning go well?"

"Excuse me, Charlotte. I can't eat until I take care of something." Bonita made up her mind that she had to register her complaint about the scene she'd just watched, and she had to do it right now. The scene came at the very beginning of the picture, and it would set the mood for the entire story. This quasi-rape that Jordan had devised would make Doug's character unlovable for the audience right from the beginning. How could even the right actor ever overcome such an obstacle? And Bonita was not convinced yet that Doug would be the right actor, even with proper direction.

Bonita began her march toward the trailer with high resolve, but then as she reviewed every unsuccessful encounter she'd ever had with the haughty adversary waiting inside for her, she began to falter. She knew that this time she must be more circumspect. She couldn't pretend to like him, but she had to try to appear to be friendly and conciliatory in order to muffle the explosion that Jordan McCaslin always unleashed when someone disagreed with him. She knocked gently on the trailer door, but in her mind's eye she was pounding on it furiously.

"Well, just look what I've attracted to my lair," Jordan said as he opened the door and took her hand to help her up the steps. She saw what he meant once she was inside the plush office that took up the front half of the trailer. It had been decorated with thick brown carpeting and wood paneling, with an upholstered banquette couch in a masculine plaid along one wall. A desk covered with papers took over one corner of the room, and through the narrow hallway she could see a small sleeping area.

"I'm just trying to get some desk work done before they bring over my lunch. I haven't seen you all week."

Jordan was being unexpectedly nice, and she tried to decide whether it was because he was putting their past quarrels behind him, or because he thought she had come to protest Brad's banishment and was putting on an innocent front. He'd been wearing a sheepskin jacket with a warm fleece lining all morning, and now it was thrown over the couch. He hurried to hang it in a narrow closet and gestured to her to sit down. When she wouldn't, he sat down himself, and regarded her through narrowly scrutinizing eyes.

"Why did you send Brad away today?" she asked, searching for a way to begin her conversation with him.

"Because this is a closed set, and if I start making exceptions, every curious bumpkin in town will be here gawking and giggling."

"Are you calling Brad a bumpkin?" she asked, feeling her face redden with consternation. "He had good reason to be here. I invited him."

"Is it so important to you that he be with you?" Jordan asked, standing up and moving close to her since it was now obvious she wasn't going to sit down with him. He was wearing a blue crew-necked sweater and she was sure she could see in his stare the exact reflection of the calm blue-water color the wool had been dyed.

"I didn't really come here to talk about that," she said. "As Brad said, you're the boss on your set."

"Well, apparently Brad has a little more sense than he lets show," Jordan said with a dismissing shrug of superiority.

"I wanted to talk with you about the scenes you shot this morning."

"What about them?" he said.

She noticed the cold tone to his voice and tried not to let it make her angry this time, but to remain as polite as possible.

"I just think the audience has to like the characters right away, to feel how sensitive and . . . and . . . gentle they both are."

"It's the kiss you're objecting to, isn't it?"

"Well, it seems so forceful. After all, he's not a worldly man. He's lived in the country all his life, he's shy."

"I'm sure in your eyes he's just about the most perfect man who walks the Monterey Peninsula."

"No, he's not perfect. He's too withdrawn, too idealistic sometimes. He has faults."

"You're so in love with this guy, Bonita, that you can't even be objective about this script. Let me tell you this about him: Even a country bumpkin should know what to do when he sees a woman like the character in your story. Sure he's shy, sure he hasn't seen much of the world, but when he sees her, he knows what to do."

Jordan reached toward Bonita to take one of her small wrists into his big brown hands, strengthened by his grip on so many tennis racquets.

"He won't let her get away without showing how he feels. But he doesn't use words." Jordan grabbed her other wrist with his free hand, and began slowly forcing her hands behind her back.

"He'll show her in a way an innocent girl will best remember." Bonita realized with alarm what Jordan was trying to do, and she began to struggle against his strength. But it was no use. He'd caught her in his trap before she'd seen it.

"He'll speak to her chaste heart directly, he'll show her with action."

Bonita struggled to avoid the inevitable. She turned her head from side to side, hoping he would be unable to find her lips. But his lips, slowly curling themselves around the sensuous words he was whispering, came closer and closer.

"And the more she struggles, the more brutal he becomes in his passion to convince her." Now Jordan was interrupting his words to kiss her neck and throat, for her head was thrown back to avoid him in any way she could.

Listening to his words as well as to the uncontrollable pulsations of her body which his lips were causing, Bonita decided to heed his warning, and she stopped her struggles for an instant, hoping he would feel he'd won the argument and let her go. Her eyes were filled with tears of humiliation as she looked up at him, pleading wordlessly for him to stop his cruel trick. But Jordan's eyes gave off an astral glow of desire that told her at once that her struggle was not over.

His lips touched hers tentatively at first, but as she resumed her struggling, he took control of her, wringing from her in the long kiss that followed every ounce of resistance, until she was limp in his arms, her hands now free of his bondage and loose at her sides.

When his mouth finally released her, she fell against him, exhausted from the emotion of the fight against him and the completeness of his physical victory over her. He held her in his arms, caressing her shoulders with the assurance of one who has been the victor in battle, and who now chooses to be merciful with the prisoners.

His hold on her now was not demanding, but reassuring, almost as if he really cared that she not despise him for what had happened. As a man of action he had used the approach most natural to him in his attempt to convince her, and she guessed that he now felt sorry he had been so forceful with her.

"You see," Jordan said with throaty persuasion,

"that was not so bad. You saw out there on the beach how Kate responded. Didn't you learn something from that?" And he kissed her again, and just as the actress had taught her, this time Bonita's arms went around his neck. But suddenly Jordan stopped himself, exerting such a control over his emotions that he stepped away from her, leaving her arms outstretched, her hands still softly touching the neck of his sweater, brushed by the fringe of his hair.

He reached up and took her hands in his, and led her gently to the couch, then he paced in front of her, as if struggling with himself in an attempt to return their relationship to one of strict professionalism. When he finally spoke, it was not about himself or Bonita, as she had hoped, but the characters in the script again.

"You see, the old legend about love is that it is somehow ennobling. It is supposed to civilize and soften a man. If we don't start Doug out as a rather rash character, then his performance has nowhere to go. We have to leave him some room to change, to grow, under her spell, or the picture won't be interesting to anyone."

"I see," Bonita said softly, and she realized that Jordan's kisses had done more to convince her than all his logical analysis of the script could ever do.

Now she had experienced for herself what she had only written about or dreamed about in the past: the overpowering mastery of a man's arms. New and confusing insights were cascading through her thoughts as she watched him aimlessly stride about his small office. She wanted to learn more from him, experience more of the wild emotion he seemed capable of bringing to the surface of her consciousness. But Jordan had made it clear he did not want to bother himself any further with her lessons in love. He seemed determined to forget what had just happened, and make her forget it as well.

He sat down behind his desk and picked up a piece

of paper that reminded him of something. "I have a new picture coming out next month. We're going to sneak preview it in San Francisco to get audience reaction. I think you might trust my judgment if you could see what I've done in that film. Doug is in it and he's wonderful."

He was returning to his more familiar impersonal methods of trying to win her cooperation, and Bonita was not sure she wanted to go back so soon to hating him.

"Why don't you come with me to San Francisco?" he asked with sudden inspiration. "My plane's at the Monterey airport. We can fly up and spend the day in the city, then have an early dinner and see the picture."

"I don't know." Bonita was put off guard by his sudden plans.

"You aren't afraid of being alone with me, are you? I promise you have nothing to be afraid of from me anymore."

She studied him closely for clues to what he meant. Was this his way of apologizing to her, or was he reminding himself he didn't dare play any further with the emotions of such an impressionable girl?

"Come on, Bonita. Don't you ever set foot out of this paradise of yours? Don't you ever do things on impulse, just because they sound exciting?"

More than anything, Bonita did want to be that kind of person, the kind who would jump at a thrilling invitation and not worry about the consequences.

"Yes, I want to come. But . . ."

"All right then, it's all settled. I'll pick you up tomorrow morning at about ten. Now, I've got to get some of this work taken care of," he said, shuffling through the papers on his desk.

Bonita wanted some sign from him, a look or a word, but he was unwilling to acknowledge that anything was changed between them. She couldn't stand being near him like this with the churning uncertainties that were distracting her.

"If you'll excuse me, I think I'll take a walk before I eat lunch."

"Walking must be the favorite pastime up here," he said impersonally, as if he were making small talk with any local citizen. "There are certainly enough beautiful places to explore."

When she turned to look at him as she stepped toward the door, she noticed that he was leaning forward with one hand on his forehead, so that his eyes were concealed from her view. Obviously he felt he had concluded his meeting with her, so without another word she left his trailer.

She saw a white-jacketed commissary worker coming toward her on the path with a large tray covered with a starched napkin, and as he passed her he gave a friendly nod. The producer apparently received special service so that he could enjoy his meals in complete privacy rather than mix with the rest of the company. Bonita could see everyone else, including the director and the stars, enjoying their festive picnic overlooking the sea.

She avoided that path and instead walked up the road to Point Joe. She went as far as she could safely go onto the rocks, and stood watching the swirl of the ocean waters, a ghostly blend of lighter and darker blues, covering the depths of wrecked ships beneath the surface just as Jordan's blue eyes concealed the wreckage of romance lost forever.

The waters here were never still, in fair weather or foul. It was said that the unusual turbulence resulted from unique configurations on the ocean floor just off this point. The swell of the ocean surged first this way, and then met opposing swells to rise up, and then push across one another. This spot was called the Restless Sea, and the longer Bonita stood and watched it, the more she felt the same crosscurrents tearing at her heart.

## CHAPTER SIX

This was only the second time she'd been shown to the chauffeured limousine, but Bonita was surprised to find that already she had learned to put on the air of a princess born to the realm. She gave the driver a smiling "good morning" as she stepped into the car and sat down beside her escort. But when she turned to look at the man beside her she suddenly lost all her composure.

The shadowed interior of the car made Jordan's skin seem tanner than ever, and she could see the glistening of his pure white teeth as he smiled at her in greeting. He was wearing a beautifully tailored suit of soft beige with a blue fleck to its weave, and he looked so effortlessly elegant that there could be no doubt he belonged in a limousine. Bonita, on the other hand, for all her attempts at casualness, still felt like an imposter in such surroundings.

They sped through the valley and then over the winding Laureles Grade Road. Within a few minutes they were driving beneath the blue arch at the entrance of the Monterey Peninsula Airport. They went down a driveway lined with pines, past the main terminal building, and toward a private parking area that required a special pass card in order to open the gate in the high fence. Their driver took them to the far end of the parking lot, right to the door of a building perched at the edge of the runway marked Del Monte Aviation.

Bonita was overwhelmed by the service they received as soon as they were inside the building. Obviously those who traveled on the corporate jets and private planes and used this waiting room expected to be treated well. A friendly man came from behind the counter and offered Bonita a comfortable chair near the window and a cup of coffee.

She studied the wide array of airplanes standing in rows just outside the window on the large concrete field. She didn't know much about airplanes, but she was impressed by the fact that every plane was so freshly painted that it sparkled in the sun. Most were white with stripes and numbers in bright primary colors for contrast.

A young girl with a knapsack was seated on the couch across from Bonita. Suddenly she leaned forward and asked, "You going to San Diego?"

Bonita was surprised by the question. "Why no. We're just going up to San Francisco."

"Well, I wish you were going to San Diego."

"Are you waiting for someone?" Bonita asked her.

"I'm waiting for anyone," she said. "Anyone who's going my way. Say, your pilot wouldn't be going south after he leaves you off, would he?"

"No, he's waiting for us. We're coming back tonight."

"Too bad. I just gotta hitch a ride south. My boyfriend is in San Diego and I promised I'd be there by tonight."

"You mean you want to hitchhike on an airplane?" Bonita asked with surprise.

"Yeah. Usually if I wait here long enough I can find some pilot going where I want to go. And most don't charge me a thing to tag along. They like to have company if they're flying alone."

"Excuse me," Jordan's imperious voice interrupted

the girl in a way that made it clear he had no time for such a person. Bonita was sorry to see the girl wander away and approach another traveler, for she had been fascinated to hear the girl describe her unusual travel technique. How Bonita envied the free spirit that carried that young girl to wherever she wanted to go, the courage that made her hop aboard any plane and take off for new places and meetings with new people.

"I thought you'd like to meet our pilot," Jordan said. "This is Paul." Bonita shook hands with the husky young red-haired man who came toward her.

"That's my co-pilot over there on FSS," Paul said, waving his other hand toward a man seated at a small desk across the room, talking on a yellow wall phone.

"What is FSS?" Bonita asked.

"That's the Flight Service Station. He's getting weather information and filing our flight plan. Everything's ready to go, Mr. McCaslin, if you'd like to come on out and get aboard."

As they walked out to the plane, Bonita whispered to Jordan, "Do the pilot and co-pilot work for you?"

"They work for the studio."

"What a terrible expense," she said as they came to the red and white miniature jetliner that belonged to Magnet Studios.

"What kind of plane is this?" she asked Paul. He was holding one of her elbows firmly, and Jordan was holding the other as she cautiously stepped up the three small steps that had been unfolded from the doorway of the plane.

"It's a turbojet Stretch Lear, a Lear 36 it's called officially."

"It must be worth a small fortune."

"It's a real honey of a plane," Paul said, scrambling into the plane after her and taking a seat up front in the cockpit where he began turning switches and checking things so that he was too busy to chat anymore.

Jordan swung himself easily up the steps and into one of the two large padded lounge chairs that took up almost half of the cabin space in the plane. There was a couch along the other wall of the plane, with a small fold-down table in front of it. She sat down in the chair next to him and began fastening her seat belt.

"Care for a drink?" Jordan asked her, opening a compartment beside him to disclose a full bar with an ice bucket that had obviously just been filled.

She wrinkled her nose critically at all the luxury around them. "This plane had to cost the studio millions of dollars."

"Do you think I have it just to show off?" he asked, a hint of irritation darkening the blue of his eyes. "Moviemaking nowadays goes on all over the world. My next picture will be filmed in Utah, and the one after that in Acapulco. This plane saves me hours of time, and time is money." When she still looked unsatisfied, he went on.

"Look, if it will make you feel any better, we charter the plane and the crew out when we don't need them. It almost pays for itself in the charter fees, so just relax and enjoy yourself, will you?" He laughed and she realized that she must sound terribly naive to him.

"I hope you haven't decided to take on the responsibility for the economic policies of Magnet Studios, with all your other duties," Jordan said, his voice gently teasing but his eyes narrowing as if to focus the attention of both of them on the very basic controversies that still divided them. Jordan could be a pleasant host when he wanted to, but he still never hesitated to show his obstinate side, to give warning that he would allow no one to question his way of doing things.

The co-pilot came on board, locked the door, and he and Paul put on their earphones and began preparing for takeoff. Bonita was too busy watching what they were doing to worry about her disagreements with Jordan McCaslin. It was a beautiful day to be flying, not as warm as the day before but still a clear and sunny spring day.

She felt the thrust of the jet engines as they lifted them from the runway and into the air over her beloved Monterey Peninsula. Bonita turned in her chair beside Jordan to peer first past him out the window on his side, and then out the window over the couch. She reveled in the experience of seeing her world from a new perspective. How small the peninsula seemed now in contrast to the enormity of the endless sea that spread out toward the horizon. And the land beyond the peninsula seemed endless as well, spreading eastward toward places she wanted to see.

It seemed like only a few minutes later that the men in the cockpit began their preparations for the landing. She remembered the times she'd driven her grandmother up to the city. Alberta loved to go to San Francisco and explore, and Bonita was always glad to take her and looked forward to the treasures and excitement that the city offered. But she always dreaded spending over an hour in the car driving through heavy traffic to get there. Now she had made the trip in a matter of minutes. She had to admit that Jordan McCaslin had won her over to his way of travel. This was the way to see the world in a hurry.

From the airport they took a cab downtown and spent the early part of the day wandering through the cluster of chic stores around Union Square, but Bonita was soon bored with window shopping. Before Jordan could summon a cab, Bonita insisted they climb onto a cable car for a ride out to the wharf.

Jordan held her tightly around the waist as they stood on the runningboard of the crowded cable car and with his other hand clutched the pole to keep both of them from falling off as the car careened up the steep crest of one hill and pitched with a crunch of gears down another.

The cars only moved nine miles an hour, the speed of the cables that rattled beneath the pavement of the street, but they seemed to fly. Then the gripman stomped on the lever that operated the wood slab brakes and clanged the bell that could be heard for miles, and with a prayer from every passenger they lurched to a stop at the intersection at the bottom of the hill.

"Do you know I've been to San Francisco dozens of times and I've never ridden a cable car," Jordan laughed.

"You can't see much from the backseat of a limousine," she said as they jumped off, and hoped almost at once that he hadn't heard her unkind implication.

Bonita was surprised to learn that Jordan had never ridden the ferry across San Francisco Bay to Sausalito either, so she suggested they take the time to do it, even if it meant hurrying through dinner later. They walked the streets of the quaint bayside artists' colony of Sausalito, stopping to watch the artisans at work in the pottery, jewelry, and leather studios along the way. Jordan pulled out his wallet several times, offering to buy something Bonita admired, but even when he pointed out a hand-tooled leather collar that might suit Lark, she wasn't interested.

"I'm afraid I'm not much of a shopper," she said.

"Then you're the first woman with that problem that I've ever met," he said, smiling at her with a real hint of sincerity.

As they ferried back to San Francisco, Bonita stood on the deck, unmindful of the wind that was whipping her hair into her face, too thrilled by the view of the now-deserted prison island of Alcatraz they were passing in the middle of the bay, and the clean white buildings of San Francisco, stacked up and down the steep hills that seemed comically inappropriate for city life. The sun was low in the sky, and it pierced at their eyes with blinking beams of reddish light as it peeked at them around the cables and towers of the Golden Gate Bridge.

Jordan had made a reservation at Ernie's, one of San Francisco's most famous gourmet restaurants, but Bonita urged him to call and cancel it so that they could eat at Fisherman's Wharf. They sat at a table right near the water, eating sourdough French bread, drinking white wine, and dipping cracked crab into a sweet mustard sauce as the bay darkened in front of them. As they were served their coffee, Bonita saw Jordan sneak a look at his watch.

"Do we have to hurry?" she asked.

"No, they're running the film at seven thirty so we have time for coffee before we go."

"I wish we could just sit here forever," she sighed, thinking of the movie she was about to see, and how difficult it would be to judge its merit with the producer sitting beside her waiting for praise and congratulation.

"You really love San Francisco, don't you?" he asked her.

"Yes, I do. There are so many people here, so close together, that they seem to strike sparks off each other. It's exciting to be in a city, it's so different from the quiet life I usually lead."

"And yet you almost turned me down when I invited you to come with me today." He leaned forward to study her, his coffee cup cradled between his two large hands, the steam rising from it so that his face seemed softened and romanticized through the vapor.

"Bonita," he said quietly, "you remind me of a bird that is dying to fly, but is afraid to leave its cage."

"I'm not trapped in a cage," she said. "I have a very comfy nest."

He seemed to notice that she was only disagreeing with a few words in his assessment of her personality, so he went on to expand his views.

"If you settle down too permanently in that nest,

you'll never get to see new things and do new things. Think of New York, New Orleans, Paris, Acapulco."

"But I love what I have at home. I have something there that no one should ever forsake."

"Something, or *someone?*" he asked, putting his cup down to watch her think over her answer.

It was true, she had been thinking about her grandmother. She could never walk away and leave forever the woman who had raised her since childhood, who had tried so hard to replace the love of a father and mother with her own love. Bonita wanted to sample the world outside her home territory. She desperately hoped that there would be exciting opportunities ahead for her, adventures that would take her to faraway places, but she felt that in between she would need to come back home to the valley and the woman who had taught her to love it. The valley, for her, meant security and love, and she couldn't live without that foundation. How awful to crave both—the stimulation of adventure and the security of love—when she would have to choose one or the other.

Now she wanted to tell Jordan how she felt, for he had been sensitive enough to recognize the ambivalence within her, and she needed to talk about it with someone. She gazed across the candlelight at him and began her explanation.

His question, **So**meone?, still showed in his face.

"You're right, you know," she said. But almost as soon as the words were out of her mouth Jordan made a move so abrupt that it startled her. With the power of a rising thundercloud he stood up from the table and began pounding his fist into the palm of his other hand.

"Where is that waiter?" he asked.

"I thought you said we didn't have to hurry," she protested, but at the same time she began getting her things together to leave, for he seemed unshakable, as usual, in his decision.

"I want to get going," he said, and he quickly paid

the check and pushed her ahead of him out of the restaurant.

Bonita was certain that he would let her continue their conversation once they were settled inside the taxi, but he seemed preoccupied as he lit a cigarette with restless fingers, so she sat silently looking out the window, watching a small pocket of spring fog as it poured up over the rim of a hill right along with their cab. She assumed he was nervous about the preview they were going to, for his picture was about to be judged by its first paying audience, so she didn't interrupt his thoughts.

"We wanted this sneak preview out of town so that we'd get an audience reaction that would be completely free of bias," Jordan said as the cab driver let them off in front of a very ordinary movie theater on a quiet San Francisco side street. "This audience has heard no industry gossip about what to expect, so we hope to take them by surprise."

Jordan introduced himself to the usher at the door who was handing out comment cards, and they went inside to take seats at the back in a row that had been roped off to reserve it.

"It's a young audience," Jordan observed as he watched people pass down the aisles to their seats. "That's because it's a weeknight. Oh, here's the rest of our group."

Jordan stood up to greet the men who were joining them in the reserved row, and Bonita smiled at several she recognized who were working on his current project in Carmel. One was a film editor, another the art director, and the ones she didn't know she assumed were studio executives who had flown up from Hollywood.

The lights dimmed and an announcement card filled the screen: A MAJOR STUDIO PREVIEW! Some of the audience cheered, some booed, and the rest rustled about in their seats getting comfortable.

Bonita tried hard throughout the picture to keep an open mind and to appreciate the cinematic skills that had gone into the production. But she found it hard to enjoy the picture because there was no character on the screen with whom she could identify. The only female was in the minor role of a nagging wife. The rest were members of a band of thieves intent upon robbing a New York City bank.

The last scene in the picture was a bloody shootout. As the members of the gang fell under police bullets, one by one, Bonita flinched each time in spite of herself. Finally, she pressed her hands over her face to escape the horror that filled the screen. Doug Driver was playing a smaller role than usual in the picture, that of the police lieutenant who had relentlessly tracked down the criminals.

Bonita peeked between her fingers to make sure the blood had stopped flowing, and then watched Doug make his final, moving speech just before the fadeout. She had to admire his performance, for he was more understated than usual, his voice quietly modulated, and his manner sincere and restrained.

Suddenly Bonita heard a harsh whisper close to her ear. "How do you expect to see my picture with your hands over your face? Is it really so horrible?"

Bonita turned to look at Jordan's face, ghostly in the flashing reflection from the movie screen. She realized she had made a fatal mistake in letting him catch her in a gesture of disapproval. For all his confidence, Jordan needed praise for his work as much as anyone else. She could tell even in the dark, from the stiffly forbidding way the man beside her was sitting, that she had made him angry, and she wanted to appease him.

"That was an exciting finish, Jordan. It got so tense I couldn't even watch." She tried to make a light laughing sound, as if the joke were on her, but she was not sure she had fooled him.

"Did you see enough to realize what a fine actor Doug can be when he's directed right?" Jordan whispered. "That's what I brought you here for."

"Yes, he was good. But how did you ever get him to play such a small part?"

"Doug wanted to play the part just because of that last speech. He wants to try new things. Now come on, we'll go next door and have a drink while we wait for the cards."

There was a neighborhood bar next door and one of Jordan's aides had hurried there ahead of them to arrange for a large table at the back of the room. Jordan introduced her to the men she didn't know, but after that everyone ignored her completely. They had ordered several bottles of champagne, and from time to time someone would lean over automatically to fill her glass, but the rest of the time they huddled over the cards that had been filled out by the theater audience and argued back and forth over what they meant.

"I've made a quick tabulation here, Jordan, and it shows 85 percent checked off *excellent*, so I think we've got another box-office smash."

"But look, here's six different people who took the trouble to write 'It drags.' That means that middle part goes on too long."

"We could cut the scene at the coffee shop."

"I like that scene."

"I hate that scene."

"That scene cost us twenty-two thousand."

"We could just shorten the scene."

The arguing stopped when Jordan finally dropped the cards he was studying and leaned back in his chair to run his hands through his hair with a tired gesture that caught Bonita's sympathetic attention.

"I've read all the cards. The reactions are good. But the coffee-shop scene has to come out. I could see that in the theater. People were wriggling and losing interest. Take it out, Jim. All of it. Everything else is fine."

"Right, Mr. McCaslin."

Now that the imperative decision had been made, the men talked in a more relaxed manner for a while, planning the schedule for the picture's publicity, the gala premiere, and the date for the release to the theaters, and Bonita sipped at her champagne and listened, impressed by Jordan McCaslin's command of all the complicated facets of his business, and his ability to maintain control of all the diverse opinions around the table.

"Thank you, gentlemen. I think that wraps it up. I have a tired lady here to take home."

Bonita's eyes flew open as she realized that the champagne had made her sleepy, and she'd been resting with her head against the back of the leather booth.

"Oh, I'm fine," she mumbled as Jordan helped her to her feet, but then she realized how hard it was to stand up, and was glad for his supportive hand.

The damp air outside the tavern felt good, and Bonita blinked rapidly and breathed in great gulps of it as they waited for their cab. The streets were deserted, so she knew the meeting had been long and that it was very late. She wondered just how much champagne she'd had, for now that the cool air had awakened her she felt unusually buoyant, almost giddy with delight at just being with Jordan McCaslin, all her arguments with him out of her thoughts.

At the airport Paul and his co-pilot were waiting for them beside the plane where the taxi left them off.

"I've checked with weather service, sir, and there's some fog at the Monterey Airport, but I don't think we'll have any trouble getting in," Paul said.

"Fog? Oh, I love fog," Bonita said. "It makes everything so beautiful and mysterious."

"It also makes the runway a bit mysterious," Paul laughed at her, "but don't you worry about it. We've got instruments."

As they settled into the snug compartment of the plane, the serious co-pilot turned to Bonita to explain the fog.

"It often happens that the day after an unusually warm day on the peninsula that airport gets foggy."

"Yeah," Paul agreed. "It's funny, Monterey is either the only airport in the area that's fogged in, or it's the only one that's clear."

"The food-service people put your order on board, sir," the co-pilot told Jordan as they both turned their attention back to the controls of the plane.

Jordan opened the bar compartment and brought out a bottle of chilled champagne and a tray of caviar and crackers.

"You see, I expected to celebrate the success of my picture," he said.

"Your picture will be a success, Jordan. I'm sure of it."

Bonita was concentrating so hard on convincing him, that she forgot her seat belt and Jordan was forced to lean across her and buckle it for her just as the plane began its swoop into the air.

"Champagne?" Jordan asked, opening the bottle as soon as they were smoothly airborne.

"Oh, I'd love it," she said.

Bonita leaned back comfortably to indulge herself in the luxury of the moment. She could not believe that she was zooming at jet speed across the skies while calmly sipping a drink with such a handsome man. This was the kind of adventure she'd only dreamed about before, and never dared hope she would be able to live out.

"It's certainly warm in here," she said. She put down her glass and took off her seat belt to remove the jacket of her new checkered suit.

"Let's sit over here where we can be more comfortable," Jordan said, and he moved to the couch.

Bonita stood up to adjust her white silk blouse beneath her brilliant green velvet vest, but she forgot that the ceiling of the plane was so low that Jordan had stayed in a crouched position as he moved across the space, and she bumped her head and lost her balance. She fell heavily into Jordan's lap, laughing as she did so and glancing up front to make sure that the crew was too busy to see what had happened.

"Well, look at the baby bird that has fallen from its nest right into my lap," Jordan said.

"I think I'll stay right here where I won't bounce around anymore," she said with a tone of mischief to her voice, surprising herself with her boldly flirtatious manner. It seemed like such fun to be teasing Jordan McCaslin. She was enjoying the look of wonder in his eyes.

"You can be my seat belt," she said, giggling. "Then I'll be safe and secure." He put his arms around her waist almost at once, looking into her eyes as if he had never seen her before.

She picked up her champagne glass and sipped happily as Jordan told her how much he had enjoyed seeing San Francisco through her eyes. And after a while they said nothing, and she sat, too content to move from his lap. Finally she put down her glass and rested her head on his shoulder. He put one hand on her hair and spoke softly into her ear, his voice steady and rhythmic as if he were hypnotizing her.

"Your hair is such a beautiful dark color that it reflects the light, and I can see all different colors in it. It reminds me of an exotic bird, with feathers containing those tropical colors that change as you look at them, so you can't tell if the color comes from the feathers themselves, or the sheen of reflection."

Bonita had never heard such words from a man before, she'd never even known a man eloquent enough to speak words so memorable that she would never forget them for the rest of her life. She lifted her head to look at him, but instead caught a glimpse of the small round window just over his shoulder.

"Oh, Jordan, look! It's foggy. We're going to have to circle for hours and hours. Maybe we'll never get to land." She snuggled into his arms, quite happy with the thought that their time together would be extended indefinitely.

"Are you afraid?" he asked.

"No, I'm just afraid we'll run out of that marvelous champagne."

Suddenly, but very gently, Jordan lifted her from his lap to the seat beside him, and he leaned across the cabin to get the champagne bottle and refill their glasses. Bonita felt disappointed, realizing she had wanted the security of his arms more than a refill of her glass.

"Mr. McCaslin, we're going to be making a two-minute turn. It's clearing to the east so we'll try to come in that way on runway two eight," Paul's voice announced on the speaker next to the bar cabinet.

Jordon didn't react right away, but sat turned sideways toward Bonita, and she could see him over the rim of her lifted glass staring into her eyes.

"I think we're landing just in time. I don't know how much more of this celebration party I could stand," he said evenly. He clenched his jaw so tightly that Bonita could see the muscles stand out like cords of steel along the side of his neck above his blue shirt collar. He moved across to his chair like a crouched lion nervously moving across its den, without giving her another look and without bothering to help her to her chair.

Bonita fumbled with the straps of her seat belt, finding them awkward and uncooperative, but she had them fastened just as she felt the dizzying deceleration of the engines for the landing.

Jordan jumped down out of the plane ahead of her, ignoring the steps. When she went to follow him she found the steps hard to locate in the dark and she held her arms out to him helplessly.

"All right, I'll catch you. Just jump to me," he said.

When she landed in his arms he hurried to set her upright, then reached inside the plane for the jacket she'd forgotten and held it for her as she slipped it on. The limousine was waiting at the edge of the runway, and though Bonita wanted to hurry through the cold she found her legs were unable to step out as surely as usual.

The headlights of the car illuminated the fog in front of them so that she could clearly see the swirls of mist ahead of her twist and curl at her feet. She stopped to watch in fascination. The runway looked like the dream sequence in a Fred Astaire and Ginger Rogers musical, and she felt as if she and Jordan should dance across the stage, but in truth she barely felt capable of walking. Jordan stopped his purposeful strides to turn back and watch her. Then he smiled with a shrug, and came back to pick her up in his arms.

"Come on, my little chickadee. It's too cold to stand around out here."

"Oh, this is just like a movie," she laughed, and then she felt him put her in the backseat of the car and get in beside her.

The car was warm and Jordan was beside her, and almost as soon as the car began moving she leaned close to him and shut her eyes, wanting only to go to sleep with her head on his shoulder. He stretched his arm around her and pulled her so tightly to him that she could feel his heart beating as quickly as her own beneath the crisp cotton of his shirt.

"We'll have you home in bed in just a few minutes," he whispered.

The chauffeur was playing a tape, and music filled

the car so that he couldn't hear from the front seat what they were saying in the back.

Bonita dreamily played with the buttons on the front of Jordan's shirt. "I want to go to your home."

"My home is far away from here in Beverly Hills," he said slowly.

"You know what I mean," she said, lifting her head to look into the blaze of his eyes. "I don't want you to leave me. I want to stay with you."

Jordan made a sound deep in his chest that was as much a groan as a sigh. "You've forgotten you're with the wrong man. You don't mean that, Bonita."

"Yes, I do," she said, but her mind was as swirled with fog as the hillside their car was slowly traversing.

Then her perceptions cleared as Jordan bent his face to hers and kissed her. Suddenly she felt wide awake and filled with his energy, as his passionate lips told her things she wanted to know. She had never felt so loved and protected before in her life. He seemed to be saying he wanted her as much as she wanted him, and she pressed herself as near to him as she could get, wishing this moment could go on forever.

But very abruptly Jordan suspended this physical communication she so craved, and all the fiery strength that had gone into his kiss was now turned to control, as he shook his head away from her and pulled himself straight in the seat beside her.

Her benumbed senses told her that something was very wrong. The world seemed cold and unfriendly as she huddled in the darkness. She was near to him, but she was lost and alone without the affirmation of his lips on hers.

"I'm sorry. I promised I wouldn't do that," he said almost to himself as he fumbled in his pockets for his box of cigarettes. Then she saw the bright flare of his lighter as he drew it close to his face. His eyes were sparkling like the sea on a moonlit night. When he turned to look at her she felt weak from the strain of trying to suppress what she was feeling.

"I think you've had enough adventure for one day," he said, smiling at her like an indulgent parent. "And quite enough champagne, too."

Bonita was grateful for the wine she'd had, and for the way it had deadened her senses to yet another rebuff from him. She knew she should be hurt, for she was usually acutely sensitive to his changes in mood. But for now all she could do was wonder why. What made Jordan McCaslin close off all lines of communication whenever she felt drawn to him?

The car lurched over the familiar bump where the highway turned into the ranch driveway. Bonita looked out the window and noticed that the air was clear here. It was rarely foggy in the valley. She could see far down the driveway ahead to her house. A light was burning on the front porch and it seemed to beckon to her, offering the sure condolence and comfort of home to replace the hollow illusion of love that had just been ripped from her grasp.

*CHAPTER SEVEN*

The next morning Bonita was awakened by the loud grinding of a semi-truck negotiating the circular driveway beneath her bedroom window. She pulled herself out of bed, grumbling inwardly as she noticed the clock on her dresser said only six o'clock.

She looked outside and saw a swarm of noisy chattering movie people preparing for the day's filming on location somewhere, slammed her window shut and pulled down the blind. As she headed back toward her bed, she tripped over a stack of her clothing left on the floor last night and hurled it toward her open closet door. Soon the yard outside was quiet, and she slept again.

"Bonita, are you awake?" Alberta called softly, then opened the door to find out for herself. "Marlene is downstairs and she wants to talk to you."

Bonita pulled a pillow over her head, wishing she could hide herself more effectively. "What time is it?" she asked her grandmother, but it was a far more musical voice that sang out the answer than she'd expected.

"It's nine o'clock, and time for you to wake up and talk to me."

"Oh, Marlene. You startled me," Alberta said, turning to see the girl who had sneaked up behind her in the doorway. "I thought you were going to wait downstairs for Bonita."

Marlene pushed past Alberta to come into the bedroom and sit down on the edge of Bonita's bed. "Come on and get up, Bonita. There are things going on today and we're missing them."

"What?"

"They're filming over at Brad's place. They've probably started already and we're not there."

Bonita pushed back the quilts and gathered her long nightgown around her. Straining with the effort to sound halfway pleasant she said, "Excuse me for a minute. I wasn't expecting company."

She slowly made her way out the door and across the hall toward the bathroom. Her grandmother gave her a loving smile and headed downstairs, apparently delighted with her assumption that Marlene and Bonita were becoming close friends. She had for years tried to encourage Bonita to see more people and develop more friendships, but Bonita was usually too busy with her ranch duties or her writing, and she'd been reluctant to spend much time away from her grandmother during her recent years of heart trouble.

Bonita drank a full glass of water, then refilled the glass and drank another. Feeling somewhat restored, she returned to her bedroom where Marlene was examining one of her pale pink fingernails that matched the pink of her skirt and sweater. As patient as a cat on the hearth, she was willing to just sit and wait for Bonita for as long as it might take before she came to talk to her.

"Where were you yesterday? Busy at your typewriter? I watched for you all day at the location. Jordan said those scenes were the most important ones of the film, and I was sure you'd want to be there to watch. After all, Jordan hasn't barred you from the set yet, you know."

"When did you talk to him?" Bonita asked.

"Oh, he called me yesterday morning before he had to leave on some urgent business. He hated to miss out on yesterday's shooting, but he said he had something important he had to get out of the way and that he'd meet me today on the set."

"But what about your job? Aren't you needed at the shop?"

"Oh, I've quit that stupid job. Jordan's given me a part in the picture. That's what he called to tell me yesterday. He was so sweet, he said my test was wonderful, and that I photograph like a dream." She fluffed her blond hair as if she were appreciating its photogenic qualities.

"I'm still so sleepy I can't think. What did you say they filmed yesterday?" Bonita asked, sitting down on the bed with an uneasy feeling that she ought to get back into it and stay there all day.

"They finished up all the scenes between Doug and Kate on the beach. You know, when the young lovers are getting acquainted. Jordan said these scenes would set up the whole mood of their relationship and he wanted them done just right. You should have seen how frantic that little director was trying to get everything on film just as Jordan had told him."

"I'm sure he'd been told exactly what to do."

"Yes, but I could tell Jordan was unhappy to have to be away all day. Come on, Bonita, and get dressed, will you? You're sitting there like a seagull on a post."

"I think you'd better go on without me."

"Oh, all right. Jordan's probably looking for me. I'll meet you at Brad's house a little later."

After Marlene had ambled slowly out of the room, Bonita went to her closet to pick out something to wear, and ugly suspicions began creeping into her thoughts in spite of her efforts to ignore them. If the scenes on yesterday's shooting schedule had been so important, why would Jordan have taken off for the day to tour her around San Francisco? They had frittered their time away playing tourist in the city, while she never realized that both of them were needed in Carmel. Was it possible that he wanted her out of the way, far from the set so that she couldn't raise any objections to the direction her story was taking?

She went to fill the bathtub and poured in several handfuls of lavender petals from the jar her grandmother kept beside the tub. She tried to let the hot perfumed water soothe her, but her mind raced on. Jordan could have flown up to the city in the evening with his staff members to watch the sneak preview; there was no need to spend the entire day in San Francisco. She remembered how enthusiastic he'd been when he'd suggested making a day of it, and how busy he'd kept her so that the progress of the filming back in Carmel was never discussed. Now she was certain that the business Jordan had complained to Marlene that he had to "get out of the way" was indeed Bonita Langmeade and her interference.

She got out of the tub and began drying herself off, working up her body until she got to her face, but as she dabbed at her cheeks they were moist again, but with bitter tears. She felt hurt and deceived, the victim of a clever and devious plan by Jordan McCaslin. It was humiliating to think he would go to such lengths to silence her, after she'd tried so hard to be subtle in voicing her disagreement with his first day of filming at Spanish Bay. But while she had stood in his trailer-office, reeling from the kiss he'd used to silence her objections, he was devising a scheme to silence her further. This was obviously a man so stubborn he would allow no resistance, no matter how courteously phrased. She was filled with disgust as she considered the lengths to which the arrogant producer would go in order to get what he wanted.

She picked up the pieces of her new suit from the closet floor to hang them up, and new and embarrassing memories came to mind with the touch of the silk and velvet. She remembered giddy feelings of fun and flirtation, and how the exhilarating excitement of the champagne and flying high had led her to dream that she was in love. How foolish he must have thought her, throwing herself in his arms, waiting so eagerly for his kiss. How he must have enjoyed his feeling of power over her, knowing that his plan had worked even better than he had hoped, seeing her so completely captivated by him that she would have ridden in the dark backseat of that limousine with him to wherever he wanted to take her. She was humiliated to consider how treacherously her body had betrayed her, reacting to Jordan's every touch like a violin in the hands of a virtuoso. Oh, why did he have to be so skilled at arousing her, at making her say things to him that now seemed so ridiculous?

No wonder he had seemed so restrained. It was not noble self-control that had made him push her from his arms. He was completely bored with her. He no doubt considered the time he spent with her as merely a nagging business assignment.

At first Bonita considered hiding out all day, safe from the torturing pain of seeing him. But then she realized she would have to begin to build her immunity to him, and that it was better to encounter him today when she was still in a state of shock than to wait until after she'd had time to review the hurt of his rejection over and over again in her mind. And perhaps if she turned up on the movie set today she could try to appear the sophisticated lady, unaffected by what had happened between them last night.

When she got to Brad's ranch she was relieved to see the movie people were all busy in a cluster near the barn. The front door of the now-yellow farmhouse stood wide open, and Bonita made a dash for it, glad that she could postpone her encounter with Jordan a bit longer.

As soon as she stepped into the living room, she felt at home. Brad had bought the house from her grandfather's estate with all its furniture, and he'd been too busy or uninterested to change a thing. She remembered every chair and table in the room from her many visits to her mother's parents here at their home during the years they were alive.

She heard a familiar voice outside and went to the front window to draw a lace curtain aside. Jordan McCaslin was in the center of a group of people, seemingly giving orders to everyone at once, his quick hands gesturing this way and that as he explained to everyone concerned how he wanted things done. He was wearing a cable-knit cardigan with a wide shawl collar, and baggy pockets into which he often thrust his fists when he didn't need gestures to make his point. How decisive he was, she thought with almost a trace of admiration in her bitterness. He never doubted that his own way was best, and that made him ruthless in seeing through his plans.

She turned sadly and went to sit on the old loveseat Grandmother Beasley had brought with her to California from the Midwest before Bonita's mother was born. Bonita always liked being in this room, for it made her feel somehow closer to the mother she barely remembered, being in the house where she'd grown up. She hoped that Brad would never make any changes inside this house.

She heard Brad's heavy steps as he bounded up into the house. When he came into the room she welcomed the sight of his broad sincere face. He was an easy person to understand and deal with, uncomplicated and accepting. It was a relief to be with a man who made every situation so simple. She never had to be on her guard, or fear that she was being deceived. She could trust Brad, for he was incapable of dishonesty.

"Hi there, Bonita. Wow, those stunt riders really know their horses," he said, throwing his hat on a chair. His face was pink with exertion. "Marti Colton has been teaching me how to fall off a horse and get back on him while he's in a full gallop."

"Now there's something I've never even thought about wanting to learn."

"What's the matter, Bonita? You don't look like your usual bright self this morning."

"I am sort of depressed, I guess."

"What's wrong? Have I been neglecting you too much?"

Bonita wondered what had given him that idea. "No, that's not it. You don't owe me all your spare time. I guess the picture I saw last night bothered me. It's Jordan McCaslin's new one and bodies were falling all over the place. I feel as if every bullet had been fired from the screen directly at me."

"Aw, come on. That can't be all that's wrong. Tell Uncle Brad what's taken the smile off your face."

He sat down beside her, and his sympathy made her brave exterior crumble. Tears welled up in her eyes in spite of her efforts to hide them.

"It's nothing. I'm just tired, I guess. I was up late last night."

Brad pulled out a red bandanna from his pocket, and putting one arm around her made a rough attempt to wipe the tears from her face.

"I don't like to see you this way, Bonita."

Through the folds of the cloth he was dabbing at her face Bonita saw someone standing in the doorway and she pushed Brad's hand away to see Jordan McCaslin standing watching them. Brad saw him too, and seemed to tighten his hold around Bonita's shoulder.

"Hey, Mr. McCaslin. We didn't hear you come in."

"Obviously. I seem to be interrupting something important."

"Bonita's been telling me about your new picture. Sounds like a real bloodbath!" Brad said.

Jordan stared at the two of them so openly and with such a cold disdain in his eyes that even Brad felt discomfited. He jumped up to his feet in an attempt to lighten the tension that he must have felt in the room but could not understand.

"Guns going off, bodies falling left and right!" Brad made an agonized shout and grabbed his side as if he'd been wounded, falling across the room in an exaggerated parody that he thought so funny that he laughed out loud. But he laughed alone.

"I thought you said you liked the picture," Jordan said directly to Bonita, ignoring the buffoonery being played out in the room between them.

"I said I thought it would be a success. That's different from saying I liked it."

"I see. And then you hurried over here to give Mr. Stark your honest opinion of my work, is that it?" Jordan asked, his voice oddly constrained.

Before Bonita could defend herself, Marlene came into the house. Holding one hand to her face dramatically she went at once to Jordan's side.

"I'm so glad to have found you, Jordan. Something terrible has happened. I was watching the filming from near the barn where you told me to stand out of everyone's way, and a branch from that tree caught on one of the cameras and came back in my face. I think my face has been scratched!"

She said the last words with as much emotion as if she'd just informed them the Mona Lisa had been slashed to pieces by a madman.

"We have first-aid equipment. I'll go call my unit manager," Jordan said.

"Ohhhhh," Marlene moaned exquisitely, both hands now caressing her cheek. "Would you look at it, Jordan?" she said.

She moved in front of him, and they stood so close that as he examined her face she rested her long graceful hands on his shoulders, tightly grabbing the collar of his sweater when the pain of her injury was too much for her.

"I've got a box of bandages somewhere," Brad said.

"I know where they are, I'll go get them," Bonita said, glad for an excuse to leave the room. She went directly to the old wooden chest in the back hall off the kitchen. Her grandmother had always kept a supply of first-aid equipment in case any hands on the ranch were injured, and there in the third drawer down Bonita found everything was still there.

Jordan was watching her curiously when she reentered the living room.

"That was quick. You seem to know exactly where everything is in this house," he said.

"I think Bonita has spent as much time in this house as Brad," Marlene said, and Bonita remembered that when they were schoolgirls they had come here together to beg cookies from Grandmother Beasley on the way home from school.

Brad broke in with a laugh. "Yes, sometimes I think it is as much Bonita's house as it is mine."

Jordan was holding Marlene in his arms but that didn't stop him from giving Bonita a contemptuous look over her shoulder. "Oh, really? How cozy," he said.

Jordan had no doubt heard by now that this house was where her mother had lived, and he probably thought it terribly childish of her to come here and spend time cherishing memories of the woman she barely knew.

Jordan applied some antiseptic to Marlene's tiny scratch, and put a small piece of gauze over it. Marlene winced and said to everyone tearfully, "I know Jordan's just as worried as I am about my face. After all, in just a few days I will have to go before the cameras, and I must look perfect."

"Don't worry," Jordan said. "You aren't supposed to be gorgeous for this part, I've told you that. We can't let you outshine our star."

"Oh, you darling flatterer! Aren't you sweet to even suggest I could compete with Kate Harrigan." Marlene's mood was suddenly jubilant.

"Tell Bonita how much you liked my screen test, Jordan. She hadn't even heard that I was going to be in the picture until I told her about it this morning."

"Apparently a lot has been going on that I don't know about," Bonita said, hoping to show him that she was now very aware of the motives behind his seductive entertainments of the day before.

"The casting of the bit parts is another of the areas where your approval is not required," Jordan answered her curtly.

Then he turned to Brad. "I came to tell you we won't need the horses until tomorrow. So you can stay in here and get back to whatever it was you were doing. We don't need you in the way outside. Now I've got to get back to work."

As he headed toward the door, Marlene hurried to fall in step beside him, linking her arm through his. "Yes, we'd better get back to the set. I'm sure Brad and Bonita want to be alone and we've interrupted them long enough."

Jordan stopped and turned to look at Bonita. "I presume you're staying here, then."

"I don't see any point in coming out to watch. After all, I missed all the film that was shot yesterday..."

"... and you have more important things to do in here," he finished her sentence for her sarcastically. "Well, if you're not too busy tonight, we'll be screening the dailies in your barn at eight o'clock. You can come and see what was accomplished yesterday."

"It's a little late to make suggestions, so what's the point?" she asked.

"I wasn't asking you for a critique, I was suggesting you might like to come and show some approval for a change."

Marlene tugged at Jordan's arm. "Well, I guess Bonita feels her work on this picture is all over. But mine is just beginning. So let's get to it, and leave Bonita to concentrate on her private life."

While Marlene had enjoyed them, somehow Brad had been completely oblivious to the sparks of dissension that had just crackled between Jordan and Bonita. As he watched the departing couple he said cheerfully to Bonita, "Since you aren't going to be busy tonight, I'll come over and keep you company."

Bonita hesitated a moment before answering. Brad's presence would be calming, and maybe it would serve to remind her of the predictable days of her past to which she now wanted to return.

"All right. I'll see you then."

"We have lots of things to talk about, you know," Brad said with a strained attempt at a smile.

Bonita started for the door.

"Aren't you going to stay and watch that circus that's going on out in my west pasture?" he asked.

"I think Jordan McCaslin has made it pretty clear that he doesn't want you or me anywhere around while he's busy creating."

"Yeah, he sure doesn't waste any time being pleasant to the people he doesn't like, does he? But it looks like Marlene has got herself red-carpet treatment from the great producer."

Bonita considered Brad's words as she walked home. Lark had come to meet her and the dog's playfulness was a contrast to Bonita's dark thoughts. Jordan had made it so obvious that he didn't like her that even Brad had noticed. Jordan wanted everyone to know he was only putting up with her presence here because she happened to live where he was shooting the picture. If he'd decided to film the picture in Hollywood, she probably would never even have been invited onto the set.

Marlene, on the other hand, after outrageously obtrusive hints and demands, had been given a screen test and now a part in the picture. Jordan had chosen to put himself in close daily contact with her, so he was obviously attracted to her. From what Kate had told her, she knew that Jordan had locked his heart to real love, but that didn't mean he didn't have time for a woman like Marlene, who would demand nothing of him except flattery and entertainment.

As Bonita neared her house, she noticed that Alberta was waiting for her, resting on the porch swing instead of upstairs in her bed where she was supposed to spend several hours a day.

"Bonita, dear, I'm glad you're home. You went out the door so fast this morning I didn't get a chance to hear about your exciting trip to San Francisco yesterday."

Bonita sat down on the steps and Lark flopped into place beside her.

"It was terrible. You wouldn't believe what a conniving person that Jordan McCaslin is! I found out this morning that he only took me to San Francisco so that I wouldn't be here to see how badly the picture is going. He spent the day telling me he was enjoying himself so much, seeing a side to the city he'd never seen before, and all the time he was playing a trick on me, laughing at me. He doesn't realize people have feelings, all he wants to do is manipulate them, move them around on strings at his command."

"Don't you think you're being a little hard on him? Maybe there's some misunderstanding. If you sat down and talked things over with him . . ."

"No, I've made up my mind. I'm staying clear of him. He's not going to make a puppet out of me."

Alberta studied her granddaughter for a moment. "You look tired. Why don't you go upstairs and take a nap? I know you got home very late. Try as I might, I couldn't stay awake to see you come home."

"I *am* tired. I think I'll try to get some sleep."

"One of the boys working out in the barn told me there's a screening or something out there tonight, and you'll want to be rested up to go to that."

"I'm not going. From now on I'm staying out of this whole project. I just wish all these trucks and people would leave our property and we could forget they ever came to town."

She stood up so abruptly that Lark was an extra step behind her, and she got in the door without him.

That evening Bonita tried hard to make her world seem as normal and content as it once had been. When her grandmother insisted upon making a chocolate cake to serve to Brad, Bonita let her do it because it was her own favorite dessert and she hoped it would cheer her up. When she dressed, she tried to make herself look happy to be expecting a caller. She put on a long Mexican-style peasant dress made of wide bands of bright pink cotton lace, and tied a pink ribbon around her dark hair in an attempt to bring out some color in her pale face.

When she was sure that it was well past eight o'clock and everyone would be inside the barn, she went downstairs and found Brad waiting for her in the swing on the veranda.

"I feel like we're sitting in Times Square," he said, sweeping his arm toward the driveway. It did resemble a parking lot tonight, it was so full of cars, and the barn beyond was so well lit that it might have been a restaurant or movie theater.

"This isn't like the good old days when we could sit out here and be so alone we could hear a raccoon washing off his dinner down by the river."

"We'll be able to do that again," she said wistfully, sitting down beside him.

"Will things be just the same?"

"Of course they will. What do you mean?"

"I'm just afraid you'll be different. I'm afraid you might get to liking all this activity. Our old quiet days might seem dull to you."

"I'm looking forward to returning to the old days," she said, hoping her words held some truth.

"That's good, because I want the old Bonita back again. The country girl, the girl who doesn't care if she ever leaves her ranch."

"Well, I won't go so far as to say I'll never want to leave here at all." Bonita knew she was hedging.

"I guess what I'm trying to say, honey, is that I'm hoping you'll never want to leave me," he said, and Bonita was surprised to hear a tremor of uncertainty to his voice that she'd never heard before.

Why was Brad acting so strangely toward her lately? He seemed to be making a terrible effort to say things to her that would change their relationship. She didn't want him to force her to say any more than she felt sincerely, so she concentrated on the motion of the old swing, hoping he would too, and that the rocking would pacify him. He sat quietly for a long time, not noticing her lack of response, apparently content just to be with her, his boots steadily pushing their seat back and forth.

Bonita thought of the calm and unruffled life she could look forward to with Brad. All she'd have to do is move her toothbrush over to the familiar house across the field and life could go on forever, unchanged. She could be safe and protected here, and maybe she would never want to leave Brad's side. Maybe she'd stay in this cage (no, that was Jordan's word!), *this nest*, the rest of her life. She could read and write and explore the world and the fascinating people in it vicariously from here. Perhaps history was repeating itself and she was falling in love with Brad just as her own mother had fallen in love with the shy farmboy on the neighboring ranch.

Suddenly Bonita felt fidgety and irritated with the dull repetition of the swing. It was putting her to sleep, and she didn't want to sleep. She wanted to look at the stars and dream of the exotic civilizations that might inhabit the planets.

She jumped up and went to the edge of the porch to study the night sky. She put her hands on the railing and leaned far over it, as if stretching to meet these mysterious heavenly bodies, yearning to experience the secrets of their unknown worlds.

"Good heavens, girl. What's got into you? You're going to fall off the porch!" Brad came over to take her around the waist and pull her back to her feet. Then he stood staring at her for several moments and she knew before he did that he was going to kiss her.

As he slowly drew closer to her she wondered why he didn't just get on with it. *When a man is going to kiss a girl, he shouldn't waste time thinking about it, he should just do it,* she thought. At last Brad seemed to have made up his mind, and taking a deep sigh as if he were wishing himself good luck, he took her into a tight embrace and pressed his mouth to hers. This was the first time he had ever kissed her in the years of their friendship.

Bonita accepted the kiss with cool objectivity, waiting for the feelings that she knew his kiss should elicit from her. But she was not responding to him. She felt no craving to make the kiss last, no desire to give pleasure back for pleasure received, no passion to lose herself in the swirlings of emotion that she had experienced in a kiss before. Then she realized that Brad's kiss was but a shallow imitation of what she desired. He could only offer her a pale and lifeless copy of the kisses she had shared with Jordan McCaslin, for Jordan had somehow been able to unleash all of her pent-up need to love with the touch of his lips.

How strange it seemed to her that a kiss from Brad would make her finally see what she had been trying not to see for so long: that she was in love with someone else! She was in love with Jordan McCaslin, and it was foolish to try to convince herself that she could ever be satisfied in anyone else's arms.

She slumped against Brad, devastated to consider what her new feelings really meant. Unfortunately, Brad was having quite a different reaction. He seemed to be feeling pleased with himself now that he had finally taken some positive action to change his long-casual relationship with Bonita.

"Now we've got our future to talk about, little bird. We've known for a long time how right we are for each other. We're already so close, it just seems natural for you and me to be married. You belong right over there in that house with me."

Bonita tried to pull out of his arms to stop him from saying more, but her motion merely encouraged him to adjust his arms more tightly around her.

"Gosh, Bonita, don't you see what I'm trying to say?"

"What you're saying is how logical it is for us to be together, and what good sense it makes. What you haven't said is that you love me."

"Oh, of course I do. Everybody loves you, Bonita. Who wouldn't love you?" And before she could stop him, Brad was kissing her again, enjoying his own boldness so much that he took no notice of her merely passive response.

The familiar creaking sound of the barn door opening and the jumble of voices that followed it gave Bonita a good excuse to break away from Brad's grasp.

"I think we're being watched," Brad whispered with a proud chuckle.

"Please, Brad. I don't want anyone to see us!"

"The way you feel about me is the worst-kept secret there is around here already," Brad said, and she looked at him with surprise, waiting for an explanation of what he meant. But Brad was looking across the yard.

Bonita turned around to see that the screening was over, people were streaming from the barn, and that Jordan McCaslin was standing directly across the driveway from them, next to the barn door, one hand on his hip and the other cupping his wide chin as he made no effort to hide his interest in the romantic scene he was watching. People bumped past him, stopping to make enthusiastic comments about the film they'd just viewed, but still he stared across at Brad and Bonita.

Freed from the confines of Brad's arms, Bonita felt lightheaded as she moved again to the porch rail. She no longer had the stifled, choking feeling deep in her chest that had frightened her during the last half hour. Her heart now felt liberated, free to fly where it belonged. The calm future she had envisioned for herself with Brad now seemed imprisoning, and she knew that Jordan McCaslin represented the more exciting future she'd always wanted.

Loving Jordan meant change and disruption, she knew, and living forever in a deliciously complex puzzle. A life spent with him would be full of unexpected squalls, but there was the promise of bright surprises of clear sky as well.

Jordan began to move away from the door, and Bonita felt faint with her love for him as he came toward her. But then she realized that Marlene Webb was ahead of him on the path and that he was following her, laughing in response to some remark she'd just thrown over her shoulder to him. Jordan's mood seemed stridently happy as he called out jokes and remarks to all those around him. Marlene walked directly to Jordan's limousine which was parked in front of the house. She looked up toward the porch and caught sight of Brad and Bonita.

"Hello, you two. Couldn't you tear yourselves away from the old porch swing to come to the screening? The dailies were wonderful, weren't they, Jordan?"

"Why should Bonita be interested in the movie version when she has the real thing," he said to Marlene, casting a sulky look at Bonita that stopped the fast pendulum that was swinging in her heart.

Marlene said something else to Jordan as she stepped into his car. Bonita couldn't hear what she said, but she saw Jordan throw his head back and give a zesty laugh. Marlene was obviously the earthy type of woman Jordan enjoyed. She was only looking for fun, with no strings attached. She wasn't interested in a serious involvement, so Jordan would feel free to indulge himself in a meaningless flirtation with her.

As Jordan got in the car behind Marlene, he spoke to her laughingly, but the words were aimed straight in the direction of the porch. "I'm sure the real-life inspiration of those love scenes we've just seen on film will be even more enthralling, and I'd love to stay and watch. But we have plans of our own for this evening."

Bonita was plunged into despair to realize that Jordan thought so little of her that he was anxious to push her with his innuendos into the arms of Brad Stark for the evening.

Her flirtatious mood on the trip home from San Francisco must have alarmed him, must have made him fear she would become a nuisance to him, so he wanted to encourage her involvement with Brad so that she would leave him alone. At this moment he was obviously happy that Bonita had not come to the screening, and that all his tactics to keep her out of his way, and out of the way of his picture, were working smoothly.

Bonita sat down in one of the nearby rocking chairs and put her hands over her face, wondering in a daze how she could be so unlucky as to discover she was really in love, and that the love was completely hopeless, both on the same night. If only she could have enjoyed for a short time the feeling of what it was like to be in love. She wanted to feast on the secret for a while, but already it had turned sour.

"What's wrong, Bonita?" Brad asked.

*"Donde no hay amor, no hay dolor,"* she whispered softly to the stars above her that now seemed so forbiddingly far away.

"What did you say?"

"It's an old Spanish proverb. It means 'Where there is no love, there is no pain.'" She understood now why her every encounter with Jordan had left her in despair.

"Are you unhappy because of me?" Brad asked, sounding incredulous to consider he might have that much effect on her.

"Brad, I don't want to discuss you and me, our

future, our friendship, any of that, until after this movie business is over. Right now I don't know how I feel about anything."

"Well, I know how you feel about me, Bonita. And I just want to make sure that you know you're important to me, too," Brad said. Bonita looked at him with shock. How could he have any idea how she felt about him? What made him suddenly assume that she was in love with him?

Before she could mull over his puzzling words any further, and try to think of what she had done lately to give him such a firmly incorrect impression, she heard footsteps on the path below, and then saw Kate Harrigan leading her husband on a detour toward the house on their way from the screening to the driveway.

"Bo-nit-a, dar-ling!" Kate Harrigan's voice seemed to savor each syllable of the words as she called out.

"Doug and Kate Driver, have you met Brad Stark?"

"Sure have, over at his spread," Doug shouted, leaping up the steps to give Bonita a flamboyant embrace and a kiss on the cheek.

Doug turned to shake hands with Brad. "How's the real-life cowboy?"

"Just fine, Mr. Driver."

"Call me Doug."

"Has this young man been keeping you too busy to come around and visit the set?" Kate asked, giving Brad an evaluating look.

"Oh, no, that's not it. Jordan McCaslin has made it clear he doesn't feel comfortable when I'm around giving criticism."

"Aren't you happy with how it's going?" Kate asked.

Bonita didn't want Doug or Kate to sense any of her doubts concerning their performance. "I have some concerns about how he's interpreting my story."

"Well, you shouldn't have," Doug said. "He's doing

a great job. You know he wants to make a great picture because he thinks its a great story."

"I'm not so sure he does. All he seems to want to do is change it."

"Now, little lady, that's hogwash. Why, he's crazy about your story. He said so when he first read it. He told me it was the most beautiful love story he'd ever come across; almost made him believe in love again, he said."

"Yes, before we left Hollywood he told us how anxious he was to meet the girl who had written it," Kate said.

"Then when we got here, he was amazed that such a sheltered young thing could have written about love the way you did," Doug said.

"Now he's got Doug tied down so tightly he can't chew up all the scenery," Kate said.

"And he's got Kate wearing such high-necked blouses she has to try acting for once to get attention," he retorted.

"So what have you got to worry about?" Kate asked.

"Just how to get along with Jordan McCaslin," Bonita said. Kate came over and put an arm around her.

"I told you he's not easy to work with." She lowered her voice melodramatically. "And I told you why. He's a very disillusioned and unhappy young man."

"So you just go ahead and show your pretty face on the set whenever you want," Doug said.

"And if you have suggestions, bring them to me, no matter what tripe Jordan gave you about it being unethical for the writer to speak to the actors. I'm not afraid of him," Kate Harrigan said, and she struck a glamorous starlike pose to indicate she was too important to be crossed, all the more effective because Bonita knew it was only a pose.

"Kate will throw a can of her diet formula at him

if he tries to give her any trouble," Doug laughed, and the Drivers headed for their red Mercedes roadster in the driveway.

Bonita found it hard to resume any kind of conversation with Brad. He seemed preoccupied, and when she suggested he leave early, he looked relieved. There had been a lot of curious moments in his evening at Bonita's, and he seemed baffled as to how to interpret them. As she watched him go, Bonita remembered that his romantic approach to her had seemed forced and unnatural, and as disconcerting to him as it was to her. She wondered what had made him act as if he thought this new manner were expected of him.

When she came into the house she saw that she had forgotten the beautiful chocolate cake her grandmother had set out for her to serve to Brad. She cut one large slice, and then opened the front door and whispered, "Here, Lark." The dog padded into the house with a look as guilty as Bonita's. She put the plate on the floor in front of him and sat leaning forward on her chair, watching the dog with a melancholy expression on her face.

"One of us might as well be happy this evening," she said, patting his neck.

## CHAPTER EIGHT

The next morning Bonita was up early to fix herself a big breakfast in preparation for what she knew would be a demanding day. As she ate, she studied the shooting schedule. The crew was going to be filming at

Brad's ranch again all day and she intended to be there for every bit of it.

During a long night, filled with short bouts of sleep and many hours of contemplation looking out the window of her bedroom into the darkness, she reached many decisions about the hopeless muddle of her life. She would have to accept the fact that she was in love with Jordan McCaslin, and that it was a love that he could never return. She would have to learn to be near him and work with him, and put her emotions into cold storage. She tried to convince herself that this could be a maturing experience. Maybe she needed this tragedy in her love life in order to finally grow up and be more sophisticated about the world and more realistic in her writing. She had already learned that never again could she allow herself the girlish luxury of letting her heart ride wild and free over foolish dreamlands. Even dreams have limits, and now she understood that Jordan McCaslin stood just outside those limits of her dreams.

She knew that the best way to submerge her own unhappiness was to throw herself into her work, and at the present time her work was to observe the filming and try to have an influence on it. Now that Kate and Doug Driver had told her how much Jordan McCaslin respected her story, she felt new optimism about the film. He had always belittled her story when talking to her about it, but obviously that was just because of his own antipathy toward her. If he could separate his feelings that way, and respect her story, while disregarding her as a meaningless aggravation, then she would learn to do the same. She would try to repress her feelings for him and deal with him strictly as a business associate, ignoring the longings inside her.

She carried a big yellow pad of paper and several pencils with her so that everyone would see at once that today she meant business. As she came up the driveway toward Brad's barn, she passed a large truck with an open side. She looked up to see two big chairs, similar to barber chairs, that were placed before brightly lighted mirrors.

"Hello, Vic," she called to the makeup man who was huddled over someone, working with his sponges and brushes.

"Bonita, is that you?" Marlene was wearing a plastic cape over her costume, and she pulled herself out from under Vic's busy hands to look down at Bonita.

Bonita could hardly recognize her glamorous friend. The billowing blond hair had been pulled to the back of her neck in a tight bun, and her face, while heavily made up, looked tired and aged.

"I have to talk to you," Marlene sputtered. "Are you through?" she asked Vic with a vicious rasp.

"Almost. We can touch you up later. You're not filming for a while yet."

Marlene got out of the makeup chair and looked at herself carefully in the big mirror as she removed the protective cape and the pieces of tissue that had been inserted into the collar of her dress to protect it from the pancake makeup.

"Thanks for nothing, Vic," she said as she left the trailer. "I've never looked worse in my life."

Vic cast a knowing smile toward Bonita, and went back to rearranging the tools of his trade, showing no apparent concern over the fact that this newcomer to the movie profession disapproved of the way he had used his talents on her.

"This is outrageous. You're the writer, you've got to do something," Marlene whispered to Bonita as they walked toward the other end of the field where most of the company had gathered. "That makeup man has made me look like an old hag. And just look at this costume."

Marlene was wearing a drab, faded calico dress, and it hung from her slender shoulders in a dismal way. Bonita realized that in all the Little Theatre roles she'd seen Marlene play, the girl had always managed to costume herself in a flattering way, and had always insisted upon applying her own makeup, so that even when she portrayed a pathetic invalid she wore her false eyelashes and rouge on her cheeks. But now she had no control over how she looked, and she was obviously not happy with the results.

"You are playing a character role, Marlene. And I heard Jordan say he didn't want you to detract from the leading lady."

"Jordan won't let them do this to me. Just wait until I find him."

Switching her attack from the author to the producer, Marlene began looking around for Jordan's trailer. "Where is Mr. McCaslin?" she demanded of the assistant director as he rushed by with a script and a clipboard of notes under his arm.

"He's setting up the next shot over where those horses are tied up."

Marlene grabbed Bonita's hand and pulled her along in the direction the young man had indicated. Bonita didn't want to seek out Jordan McCaslin first thing this morning, but then she decided that maybe this was the best way to establish contact with him and let him know she was here, using Marlene as a shield. But Marlene had other ideas, and they included using Bonita as her own shield.

"Hello, dear producer," Marlene crept up behind Jordan and made a breathy whisper near his ear, startling him. He had just dismissed the actors from the scene he'd been rehearsing, and was seated in a canvas director's chair with his name on it studying his script.

"I know we're interrupting you, but Bonita insisted on talking to you about something and she says it can't wait. Tell him what you think of this costume, and this awful makeup, Bonita."

This was just the kind of direct confrontation that Bonita had planned to avoid. Marlene was putting her in the position of interfering again, and in an area where she had no business commenting. Jordan's eyes when he looked up at Bonita clearly reflected his irritation.

"You don't think Marlene looks like the schoolmarm you had in mind?" Jordan asked.

"Oh, that's not it," Bonita groped for words. "It's just that Marlene feels she looks too, well, haggard."

Jordan stood up with a sigh and went to take a close look at Marlene's face, holding her shoulders to turn her face to various angles in the sunlight.

"This face could never look haggard. No heavy thinking or self-doubt have ever marred its perfection with worry lines. These high cheekbones of yours stand out better than ever with this character job Vic's done on you."

"But Jordan, darling, when you were coaching me last night you said I should try to project warmth and deep understanding. How can I do that when I don't feel that I look my best?" Marlene cooed, holding him around the waist intimately so that he kept his hands on her shoulders.

"You can do it because you're an actress, my dear," he said, coaxing her with a slight hug.

"You're so persuasive, darling," Marlene sighed. "I think you could talk me into almost anything."

Bonita couldn't watch them anymore. She turned away and began making notes on her yellow pad.

"I hope I've convinced you on this," Jordan told Marlene. "Because you must leave your makeup and costume just as they are. If you're a professional, you know that. Now I have to get ready for the next shot."

Bonita jumped when she felt Jordan put a casual hand on her shoulder. It was like a key unlocking a treasure chest of remembered responses. She turned to look at him, hoping she could maintain her attitude of remote calmness. He seemed to want to say something to her, but he held back whatever cutting comment was on his mind and turned back to the scene he was scheduled to film.

As they walked away, Bonita assumed that Marlene had been won over until she said, "I'm going to my dressing room and fix this awful dress. I have some safety pins in my purse. If I can just tighten up the waistline, maybe I can make it fit a little better and no one will ever know."

The entire farmyard was quiet for a moment, then as soon as the scene near the horses was completed, everyone began moving to set up the next shot. Bonita put her notebook down on a table next to the commissary truck and started to fix herself a cup of coffee. Then she looked across the field toward the corral and saw Brad and Marlene sitting on top of the fence, laughing and talking together. She wondered why Marlene had decided against fixing her dress herself, and she headed over toward the couple to ask her.

As she drew closer, she realized that although the girl was wearing the same dress as Marlene, and had an identical blond chignon at the back of her neck, there was something different about her. She was speaking rapidly, grabbing Brad's hand in a friendly way as she made her point, and when she kicked her feet out from the fence rail with a burst of good humor, Bonita noticed that she was wearing heavy boots beneath her dress.

"Marlene, I'm glad you changed your mind about the dress," Bonita said as she walked up to them.

"So she fooled you, did she?" Brad laughed. "This is Marti Colton, the stuntwoman I was telling you about. She's going to double for Marlene so she's dressed up just like her."

When the girl turned toward Bonita she had a wide

smile on her freckled face, and the illusion that she was identical to the placid Marlene was immediately dispelled.

"Marti, this is Bonita Langmeade. I don't think you've met her."

Marti jumped down from the fence at once, her smile disappearing as she did so. "Oh, howdy do, Miss Langmeade. I was just asking Brad here about the horse I'm going to use. Well, excuse me. I don't want to interrupt you two." She hurried away so fast that Bonita was disappointed. Brad obviously admired the girl, and she wanted to get to know her better.

"What's the matter with her?" she asked Brad. "She acted as if I caught her doing something awful, the way she wanted to get away from me."

"Maybe she's afraid you'll be upset, finding her talking with me."

"Oh, Brad. Don't be silly. What would give her that idea?"

"You know how people talk," he said, studying his booted feet.

Marlene was just coming out of her trailer, and Bonita smiled as she saw Marti pass by her, the two of them looking like twins in their matching costumes. Marlene's unamused eyes swept over the girl for an instant, then she continued on toward Bonita without speaking to Marti.

"I've got to find that director. I want to know how my scene is going to be staged. Come on, Bonita," Marlene said, acting as if this was of urgent concern to Bonita.

"See you later, Brad," Bonita said as she tagged along again with her friend.

They found Dan Evans near the ranch house. "Your first shot will be in this buggy," he said to Marlene.

"I hope you don't expect me to ride in a horse and buggy. My hair will get all blown around and my makeup will be dusty. Mr. McCaslin won't stand for that."

Dan gave a patient sigh, as if such selfish objections from his actresses were quite routine. "You won't have to ride. We'll have Marti double for you when the buggy comes galloping toward the house. All you have to do is sit here in the buggy and do your two lines with Kate. Someone will be holding onto the horse just out of camera range. You won't have to move an inch."

"When do I get my rehearsal?"

"We'll get to your scene in about an hour," he said. Then he pointed toward the far end of Brad's property. "We've got a tricky scene to shoot on horseback down the road there first."

"How many closeups will I have?" Marlene asked, but Dan was already walking away and didn't hear her. He knew better than to hang around a demanding bit player and discuss his plans for shooting the scene.

Bonita looked where Dan had pointed and saw that Brad was helping ready the horses. Doug Driver and several costumed extras were already up on horseback, and a camera on a wheeled dolly truck was getting into position to follow them on a fast ride down the old road lined with eucalyptus trees that led toward the river.

There were rows of old trees like this cutting haphazardly all across California. Planted as the demarcation of now-forgotten property lines or as windbreakers for farm fields no longer harvested, they now stood like lonely sentinels, guarding dirt roads that led nowhere.

"Help me up here, Bonita," Marlene said, and she climbed up into the black leather seat of the buggy. "You there," she called to a stagehand nearby. "Hold onto this horse, I don't want him moving around while I'm rehearsing."

The stagehand didn't bother to point out that the horse was tied to the fence rail, but came over to stand by the horse resignedly, apparently deciding he might as well stand around and wait near the beautiful blonde as anywhere else.

Bonita looked up to watch Marlene mumbling her lines to herself under her breath, trying out various gestures and intonations for emphasis. A few strategically inserted pins had given her dress just enough fit to accentuate her curves as she had wanted. She had even sneaked a bit of eyeliner onto her upper lids so that she now looked quite beautiful, the severe hairdo and the pale lipstick drawing attention to the sculptured beauty of her face just as Jordan had predicted.

Bonita was distracted by the loud clatter of several horses as the rehearsal began over on the road. Jordan and Dan were now on horseback, too, so that they could stay just behind the actors. The entire group galloped at top speed down the road, the incongruous black camera equipment sneaking along on quiet rubber tires behind them. Suddenly the whole group pulled to a stop, roiling a cloud of dust, and Doug was turning to speak to the other actors. Bonita tried to remember her script. She couldn't recall having written any speeches for Doug to deliver during this bit of action.

"Marlene, where's your script?" she asked.

"I don't need my script," Marlene said. "I've learned all my lines perfectly."

"I just wish I knew what was going on down the road there," Bonita said.

"Would you look at this? I've busted a fingernail getting into this silly buggy," Marlene said. "Help me down. I've got to get this fixed before they get to my scene." Marlene hurried off toward her dressing room and the bored stagehand wandered away to the coffee truck to while away his waiting time there.

Bonita paced back and forth with frustration. Had Jordan added some lines to her script? What was Doug saying to the other men, turned sideways in his saddle halfway down the road? Jordan was shouting instructions at him through the megaphone of a portable PA system in his hand, and they were repeating some of the action again, so she was sure this was a planned scene. But even the amplified voice of Jordan McCaslin was out of her hearing. If only she had a horse, too, she could ride up closer to where they were filming and hear what was going on. She aimlessly walked to the front of the buggy and patted at the tawny chestnut head of the horse tied to the schoolmarm's buggy. Then it occurred to her that there was a way for her to get close to the filming.

Bonita carefully untied the horse from the fence railing. She recognized the animal as one that Brad called Sugar Eater because it was his favorite and he pampered it with lots of his special attention.

She was wearing culottes with wide legs so it was easy to step up onto the high seat of the carriage. She took the reins in hand confidently, for although she hadn't had any experience with a buggy, she had ridden horses all her life and she knew Brad's horses were all well trained.

She made a clicking sound and gave a gentle tug on the right rein, and the horse began to move away from the fence and across the field. Bonita knew that the carriage she was riding had been rented in Hollywood and brought up here as a prop. It seemed to be a real antique. She could see old horsehair poking its way out of a hole in the stiff black leather of the seat.

"Where are you going with my buggy?" Marlene called to her as Bonita creaked slowly past the row of dressing-room trailers. Marlene had just come down the steps of her trailer and was waving one hand through the air to dry some fresh nail polish.

"I'll bring it right back. I'm going to see what they're doing down the road there."

"Wait for me," Marlene called, but Bonita was already well past her.

Bonita found it easy to direct the horse, and she crossed him over the smooth field, and through a break in the fence toward the rough open turf of the pasture. She planned to pull up on the other side of the row of trees so that she could hear the scene that was being filmed without being observed.

As Bonita looked down on the gleaming brown back of her horse, she realized that her carriage seat gave her a higher viewpoint than she'd ever had while horseback riding. It was a majestic feeling to be seated atop a carriage, riding across the countryside on such a beautiful day. She clicked a sound of encouragement to her horse, and followed it with words of praise, for she was delighted that Brad's pet had so quickly adapted to pulling a harness.

Hearing her voice the horse quickened his step just a bit, obviously enjoying just as much as Bonita the feeling that they made quite a handsome picture, traveling in their old-fashioned way. She was glad she had impulsively decided to kidnap the horse and rig. She would not only be able to find out what Jordan McCaslin was up to, but the new experience of riding in a buggy had already raised her spirits considerably.

Bonita was traveling parallel to the road, and she looked over to see that she was almost even with the spot where the crew had stopped to set up their shot midway down the road. She guided her horse closer to the eucalyptus trees where she hoped to be able to hear the megaphoned voices.

The technicians had set up a row of sun reflectors along the road, so that the sunlight could be directed toward the actors who were obscured in the shade between the tall trees. One technician was working with the stand of a reflector, using a wrench to loosen a frozen bolt so that he could twist the reflector where it was needed.

As the bolt suddenly jerked free, the reflector swung crazily on its stand, sending a dazzling reflection of sunlight toward Bonita, as bright and blinding as a full view into the sun, and startling in its suddenness. Bonita blinked quickly and, realizing what had happened, recovered at once. But the horse to which she was fastened could not know what had caused the sudden explosion. He was not as used to moviemaking equipment as the horses used in Hollywood for filming, and the sudden assault upon his senses made him rear back in terror.

Pulling back he encountered the buggy harness which was also unfamiliar and somewhat frightening in its confinement. Bonita immediately sensed the horse's panic, and she called out words of calming reassurance, but they came too late. The horse had decided on flight as his only means of escape from the trap he was in, and he began to run.

Bonita was not worried. She had the reins firmly in hand, and she began pulling back on them, gently at first, but hoping that after a few paces the horse would relax a bit and she could pull him into control. But she remembered hearing that once a startled horse has begun its flight, it runs to exhaustion, and Bonita soon realized that she was in for a harrowing ride. She tried to recall how she'd seen harness-race drivers position their bodies on their rigs for the greatest amount of stability, and she moved her feet wide apart and pushed them onto the wooden platform under her.

She called out to the horse in her loudest voice now, hoping to make herself heard over the snorting sounds of his hard breathing. Although it was obvious that the horse was not responding to her cries, she was dimly aware of a commotion on the nearby road, and she was embarrassed to think that her plight was being observed by the movie crew, causing an interruption in their work.

Why, she asked herself, had she been so foolish as

to take a novice buggy horse out for a ride, when she had no experience at this sort of thing either?

The horse was trying to put distance between himself and the ominous reflector on the road as fast as possible. He was also trying in vain to outrun the buggy that was fastened to his breast collar, so he increased his speed, switching gaits into a gallop that rocked the buggy with tipping motions that threatened to pitch Bonita out of the seat at any moment.

She felt herself slipping across the slick leather seat of the carriage. Her hip bounced painfully against the metal handrail on the edge of the seat and then she started sliding in the opposite direction. A soft clod of dirt flew off one of the horse's flying hooves and into Bonita's face. She shook her head into the wind to get the dirt out of her eyes.

Since she could not control the horse's speed, she made an effort to steer him in the safest direction. He was heading straight out across the meadow. From the sound of his feet Bonita noticed that as they drew closer to the river the soil was more firm, for no soft grasses were growing here. There were occasional rocks and boulders that had been tossed up during years when the river ran high.

She knew that the horse had a sense of self-preservation that would keep him away from the larger rocks, but he had not been trained to consider his vehicle and passenger, and sometimes he darted to change direction, throwing her buggy up against a sharp obstacle. She pulled on the reins so hard that the skin on her hands felt raw. She pleaded with herself for more strength, for stronger hands, so that she might be able to pull the horse's head back and force it to slow down. But the more she pulled, the faster her strength ebbed away.

She heard the old wheels of the buggy beneath her strain and creak, and she wondered how much longer it would stay in one piece. But she was too busy fighting for control of the horse through the thin reins to have time for any vivid mental pictures of what might happen to her. Her heart was beating rapidly and her breath was uneven, but she did not let fear get a grip on her mind.

From the corners of her eyes she saw that the boulders that were flashing by on the ground around her were becoming larger, and then she looked ahead and saw one as big as a standing man, directly in the path the heedless horse was taking. She could see from buggy height that if the horse veered to the right he would plunge directly into the ravine that sloped downward from a patch of brush, and such a fall would injure the horse fatally. So, forgetting the right rein, she put all her strength into pulling on the left one, making a last-ditch effort to save the horse from its headlong flight into possible destruction.

When the horse was only a few dozen paces from the rock, and was faced with the decision of which way to bolt, he must have felt the persuasion of Bonita's hands, for he broke stride and charged to the left so suddenly that the buggy wheels could not adapt in time. Bonita felt the sickening snap of the leather traces that had held her carriage to the horse. The horse turned, but she and the flimsy vehicle beneath her rolled forward toward the big rock. Bonita's hands flew up to her face and she screamed at the rock to move out of the way. Then with a last instinctive gesture of protection she wrapped her arms around her head and bent her face forward toward her chest.

She felt like an adagio dancer tossed into the air by a careless partner, for she was thrown up off the seat as the carriage splintered against the rocks. Then the impact of the rock under her feet jolted her, and she pulled more tightly into her curled-up position as she rolled forward across the top of the rock in an airborne somersault, and then fell off the back side of the rock, crashing down into a pile of small boulders that had chipped off the larger one during its geological lifetime.

Suddenly everything was still and quiet. It seemed strange to her that she was seeing a skyful of stars overhead and she wondered how night had come so quickly. The stars were more sparkling and beautiful than any she had ever seen before, and she felt as if she were watching a night of falling stars as their bright glow slid gracefully across the horizon. When she shook her head slightly, all the stars jumped back to their original positions and began their ballet against the velvet backdrop all over again.

She felt a vibration in the earth beneath her, and then heard the sound of horses' hooves coming toward her. Someone was coming to look for her, but would they ever find her in the dark? She wanted to call out for help, and though she tried hard to form words, she was only able to moan with an anguished sound that frightened her even more. The dance of the stars had stopped, and now she was looking only into a dark and terrible sky.

Footsteps came closer to her, rustling through the dry weeds, and she tried to sit up to meet them. There were sharp rocks under her and they were piercing her head and shoulders painfully.

"Lie still, don't try to move," a heavy voice said, and she wished she could see who it was. If only it was Jordan! He would know what to do. He would help her.

A hand gently cradled her head, and the rock that had made such a poor pillow was disentangled from her hair and pulled away. Someone was carefully brushing dirt from her face, and as his hands brushed across her eyelids she realized that her eyes were closed and that she was powerless to open them.

"You damn little fool, look what you've done to yourself." Though she could see nothing, she could hear Jordan's voice clearly. The words he spoke were harsh, but the sound was as soft as a sob. She wanted to open her eyes to see him, she needed the strength and assurance she knew he could transfer to her with one flash of his eyes. But before she could make the effort, she felt him place one hand across her forehead and his lips brushed hers in a kiss to which she could give no response.

"My darling, why do you care so much? Why can't you stay out of this and just trust me? This should never have happened!" Jordan said to her. He must have believed she couldn't hear him, and yet he was speaking to her with an urgency, as if there were things he had to tell her. "If you are hurt, I will never forgive myself. Please open your eyes and look at me, Bonita."

At his command she was able to open her eyes for the first time, and she blinked as she realized it was still a bright day, and the light bursts she had seen were not heavenly bodies at all. Now stars were glistening in the glow of Jordan's eyes.

She tried to smile up at him, content to have him near her, and sustained from any fearful thoughts of what might be wrong with her by his very presence. Now that she could see his face so full of love and concern close to hers, she wanted him to kiss her again, and she lifted her shoulders to raise herself to him. He put one arm beneath her head, but with his other hand he pushed her gently back down.

"My God, don't move. You may have a back injury."

Even through her pain, Bonita could feel the messages of fright and concern Jordan was sending her as he held her in his arms.

"I told them to call for an ambulance. It will be here soon. Don't be afraid," he whispered to her.

She wished she could tell him that she was not afraid as long as he was with her. For the first time in her life she felt loved and protected and she realized this was what she had always been seeking. Her security and her feelings of belonging were not in the Carmel Valley, but in the arms of Jordan McCaslin, wherever he might be.

She could see in his face a full return of her love. For once his face was relaxed and open, he was letting himself love. She knew he had a need to trust someone, and to love, and now she felt confident that she had broken through his cynicism, and shown him how it felt to care about someone.

Far away the sound of an ambulance siren called to them from the mouth of the valley. As that sound grew louder, she heard the sound of more horses approaching, and people's voices. She heard Doug come riding up like a movie hero and jump off his horse.

"Is she all right?" he asked Jordan.

"She's conscious, but she hasn't said a word," Jordan answered.

"That chestnut sure gave her a buggy ride she'll never forget," Doug muttered.

"Here comes the ambulance. I told Brad Stark to lead them to us," Dan Evans told Jordan breathlessly as he came rushing toward them.

Jordan started to stand up to look, but Doug had noticed Bonita's hand grasp out toward him, and he said to Jordan, "You just stay there and hold tight to that little lady. See there, she smiled! She's going to be all right."

Dan Evans was standing with one hand shading the sun from his eyes, looking toward the ranch house. "They're having a terrible time driving across the dirt."

"Well, we can't move her, so you just see to it that they get here as fast as they can," Jordan snapped, and he turned back to brush the hair from Bonita's face, as if to tell her that he was taking the best care of her that he could.

Bonita watched with somewhat blurry vision as a

blond girl in a calico dress rode up at top speed and jumped off her horse. She was touched at first to think that Marlene would rush out here to be with her, until she saw the girl pull the blond hair off her head all in one bunch and throw it down impatiently, revealing her own short brown curls beneath the wig. Then Bonita realized it was actually Marti Colton, busying herself with moving back the people and the horses.

Bonita heard Brad's voice, louder and more assertive than usual, as he rode up with the ambulance. "Where's my girl?" he shouted.

Jordan slowly removed his arm from under Bonita's head, then stood up with a more abrupt movement. "What's wrong with that crazy horse of yours, Brad? This would never have happened if he'd been trained right."

"That horse never saw a Hollywood buggy before," Brad said.

Doug Driver stepped between them as if he were the sheriff at a showdown. "Now, boys, this is no time to be arguing. Both of you step back and let the stretcher through."

The white-coated ambulance attendants with their modern equipment seemed out of place among the horses and costumed actors. Bonita observed the scene with a dazed feeling of being far away from it as they checked her over and planned how to lift her into the ambulance.

Brad kept hovering over them, asking questions and acting on her behalf as if he were an official member of her family. Apparently he had felt encouragement from having worked up the courage to kiss Bonita the night before, and felt he must play the role of suitor now that she was injured.

As she was lifted into the ambulance, she heard Brad asking, "Where's my horse? Marti, go see if that horse is okay. He's one of my real favorites."

Jordan McCaslin was standing nearby, and as the

attendants prepared to close the ambulance doors he reached out and stopped them.

"Get over here, Mr. Stark. Bonita needs someone with her. I'm sure you're the best one to console her."

"Oh, sure. But listen here, Mr. McCaslin. Don't you try to put the blame for this on my horse. He's a fine animal, and ..."

"Get in!" Jordan commanded.

While Brad leaped up into the ambulance to crouch on the small seat beside the stretcher, Jordan leaned inside to stare at Bonita, his face white with strain. She wanted to call out to him, to ask him to stay with her, but Brad was asking her how she felt, and the doors of the ambulance closed with a slam before she could utter any words.

## CHAPTER NINE

Bonita was kept at the hospital with a NO VISITORS sign on her door for two days. The first day Alberta came and sat with her for many long hours, until her own doctors insisted she go home. The strain of waiting for the results of all the tests obviously tired her. On the morning of the second day Alberta came into the room with her knitting bag, prepared to keep her granddaughter company again.

"Please don't stay here," Bonita pleaded after they'd had a short visit. "The doctors have told you there is nothing wrong with me."

"But I don't want you sitting here brooding by yourself. You look so unhappy."

"I'll be all right. You go on home and take a nap.

You have to be back at three to check me out of here and take me home."

Bonita shooed her out of the room. She needed time to think about all the baffling questions that had been swimming through her dazed brain since the accident.

What had made Jordan pull back from her just when he seemed to be allowing himself to feel something? He should have realized that all the fear he'd shown as she was lying injured meant that he cared for her. But instead he had thrown her into Brad's arms, insisting Brad ride with her to the hospital and take over her protection.

Had he noticed Brad's obvious affection for her and his recent attempts at romancing her? But Jordan McCaslin wouldn't let that stand in his way. Surely he wasn't just being gentlemanly, standing on the etiquette of the situation and letting the man who had known her the longer take precedence over him. That would not be like him. If he wanted to give in to his feelings for her, he would be here now. He would barge right into her room and take possession of what he wanted. But so far he had not even telephoned. No, the man's heart was impenetrable. The vow he'd made to never again let himself love anyone was a barrier that even her fierce desire for him could not break through.

Late that afternoon her grandmother came and drove her home. When Bonita walked into her bedroom, she had to laugh. The chest of drawers, the dressing table, even the wide windowsill, were all crowded with expensive bouquets of flowers.

"This room looks like a flower show. Look at these roses from Kate and Doug Driver. They have the longest stems I've ever seen," she said. She flipped through the rest of the cards. One was from Dan Evans, another from Vic and Charlotte, there were even flowers from Brad.

Some wild flowers gathered by hand had a card affixed to them saying, "Leave the stunt riding to the professionals. Get well soon. Marti Colton."

Then she noticed one cold white card engaved with the Magnet Studios logo. At the bottom of the card Jordan McCaslin's name and title were printed, and over them he had scrawled his initials.

"Which one came with this?" she asked her grandmother.

"This darling bowl of bachelor buttons. Have you ever seen so many in one place?"

As Bonita looked at the round mass of small blue flowers, they brought something familiar back to her mind, and then she realized that they looked exactly like the silk flowers that had been twined around her hair for the party at Jordan's house. Those were the flowers he had helped her take off when she'd been so angry with him that her fingers had botched the job. Now she put her hand to her hair absently, remembering the moment. What a cruel coincidence that some florist should have chosen those flowers to send in his name!

"Blue goes well with my bedspread. Let's put these on my bedside table," she said.

"Now you just get into bed. I'll take care of it," Alberta said, giving Bonita a steady look as she brought the flowers and placed them beside her. Bonita wondered if her grandmother had guessed the significance of that particular bowl of flowers, for she sat down on the edge of the bed and held Bonita's hand, giving her a sadly attentive look as if she understood that Bonita had committed her heart to an uncaring keeper.

"Now you try to sleep for a while. The doctor said you are to get as much rest as possible." Alberta gave her hand a squeeze.

"I don't feel tired, Grandmother. I feel too restless."

"I understand your restlessness."

"You do?"

"You know, it's amazing that you wrote with such understanding about your mother and father, because you are really not very much like them. For better or for worse, you're more like me. Your mother and father were content to stay in one place as long as they were together. But I've fought off a craving for adventure and excitement my whole life."

Bonita looked at her with surprise.

"Who do you think it was that talked your dear grandfather into pulling up stakes and leaving the family feed business in Pennsylvania to come with our son all the way out here to California? And if he'd lived a while longer, I was planning to talk him into lots more travel. I wanted to see Hawaii, Japan, Africa, even if we could only afford to go by freighter. So you see, Bonita, I understand your restlessness, your need to explore and meet new people. You got all that from me. I may appear to be a homebody, tied to her land, but it was circumstance that kept me here, not my own choice."

"Then you don't think I'm crazy to want so much out of life?"

"No, I do not. And what's more, I want you to see that you get it. But for now, you rest and dream," she said and she left the room.

Bonita turned on her side, gazed at the bowl of flowers, and soon fell sound asleep.

When she awakened, it was dark outside, and she could hear the sounds of voices and cars in the driveway. By now it seemed almost routine to have the movie company trooping around the property every evening on the way to the barn for the screening of the dailies. Bonita slipped on a robe and went downstairs.

"And what are you doing out of bed, young lady?" her grandmother asked.

"I'm hungry, so I thought I'd come down and make an omelet or something."

"If an omelet is what you want, that's what you'll

get. But I'll fix it. You just sit down here at the table."

Her grandmother had waited to eat supper with her and the two ate their cheese and onion omelets together, watching through the window as the latecomers hurried toward the barn.

"After you've eaten I want you to comb your hair and put on some lipstick. You just may have some visitors this evening," Alberta said.

"What do you mean?"

"I've had to chase Brad out of here with a broom for two days, he's been so anxious to see you. And all these movie people have been asking about you. Someone is bound to drop in after the screening."

"I don't want to see anyone."

"Not even Brad?"

"Especially Brad."

"If he comes by, I think you should talk to him. He feels very guilty about the fact that his horse ran away with you. And it might cheer you up to talk to a young friend. The doctor said you could have visitors now."

Bonita dragged up the stairs and did as her grandmother had suggested. It was a warm evening, so she opened the bedroom window. She could hear the squeak of her grandmother's rocker. She knew she was sitting with her knitting on the veranda just below the window. That was the way Alberta loved to spend the spring and summer evenings.

She took three pillows, all covered with the hand-embroidered pillowcases her grandmother had made so many years ago, and stacked them behind her so that she could sit up and read, but she found after a while that she was merely turning the pages of the book on her lap, paying no real attention to what she was reading.

Bonita was surprised when she heard a voice call out to her grandmother, for she hadn't yet heard enough commotion outside to indicate that the screening was over. The voice had a familiar sound of assurance that made Bonita drop her book and listen intently.

"Good evening, Alberta. You look like you could use some company."

"I wouldn't mind entertaining a gentleman caller, if that's what you have in mind, young man," Alberta said with a friendly laugh in her voice.

She could hear Jordan's footsteps as he came up onto the porch and soon another rocking chair joined the cadence of squeaks.

"Aren't you supposed to be watching your film?" Alberta asked.

"I've seen enough to know it's going well," he said with a sigh. "I decided I needed a walk."

Bonita pushed back the covers and went carefully across the room toward the window. She had a compulsion to listen in on the conversation below, but she didn't want to be observed, so she stood to the side, hidden behind her curtains.

"I'm glad to know you're happy with how your work is going," Alberta said. "I want you to know that I can take full credit for this movie if it is a success," she teased.

"Oh. You can?" Jordan asked her.

"If it weren't for my nagging, Bonita never would have tried to sell that story. In fact, I don't think she would have written it if I hadn't told her the story over and over."

"You told her the story?" Jordan asked, and Bonita could hear the change of sound as one rocker came to a stop.

"I don't know if you knew this, but Bonita's parents were killed when she was just a little girl," Alberta said, starting on a story.

Bonita clenched her fists with frustration. She wanted to stop her grandmother from telling Jordan any more about their family, for she knew he couldn't possibly be interested. But the warm evening air, and the knitting that moved through her fingers at a steady pace, had apparently put Alberta in a confessional frame of mind, and her low country voice continued to speak, with Bonita catching only a few words now and then.

Bonita heard a car drive up and then with relief took a peek to see Brad Stark coming up the front walk. Maybe his appearance would put a stop to Alberta's talkative mood.

"I've come to see my little Bonita. How is she tonight?" Brad asked Alberta as he took the steps two at a time. "Oh, hello there, Mr. McCaslin. I thought you'd be busy meeting with all your people over there in the barn tonight."

Jordan must have ignored him completely, for the next thing Bonita heard was her grandmother telling Brad to go on inside.

"There's coffee in the kitchen, Brad. Why don't you take a cup for yourself, and take some up to Bonita?" Alberta called.

There was a slam of the front screen door, and then Bonita heard Jordan's voice, filled with the irritation he always showed over any encounter with Brad.

"Go on with what you were saying before he interrupted you."

"Oh, where was I? Let's see now . . ."

Bonita hurried back to her bed to avoid being caught at her eavesdropping. She grimaced as she adjusted herself beneath the multicolored quilts on the bed, wishing there was some way she could hear what Alberta was saying, or warn her not to talk so much to Jordan McCaslin. Anything she told him would just give him new feelings of contempt toward Bonita and the simple story she'd written about the love affair that had ended too soon.

"Don't you look pretty, sitting there in your pink lace and ruffly stuff," Brad said in a loud voice from her doorway. "You want some coffee?"

"Thank you. Put it here on the table."

He was awkwardly juggling a full cup of coffee in each big hand.

"Did you get my flowers?" he asked. Then he looked around the room. "Oh, you got a lot of them," he said disappointedly.

He pulled the small chair from her dressing table over to the side of the bed and sat down, dwarfing it with his heavy frame, and began to ask a lot of questions about her time in the hospital. Bonita tried to answer logically, but she kept pausing, hoping she could hear some of the words being exchanged outside her window. All she could tell was that Alberta and Jordan were still talking.

"I'm coming over here tomorrow morning and take you for a ride," Brad was saying.

"You are?"

"Your grandmother told me that by tomorrow you can leave the house, and I don't want you rushing right back to that movie set. I know you'd rather be with me."

"Oh, Brad, I just want to be alone tomorrow."

"I won't take no for an answer."

Bonita paused again, listening for sounds at the window, and Brad assumed she had agreed to his plan. He drank his coffee looking very content with himself. Bonita thought she heard changes in the sounds outside. She could hear a few voices near the barn, so the screening must be over, but the porch seemed to be still now.

She picked up her own cup with a sigh, picturing Jordan McCaslin striding back to the barn to give orders to his film editors, telling them exactly how he wanted them to edit the day's film into the rough cut of the picture they were putting together piece by piece as it was filmed. She heard footsteps on the stairs and looked toward the doorway expecting to see her grandmother, but almost dropped the coffee cup with surprise when she saw Jordan McCaslin come into her room.

"Well, Brad. How neighborly of you to come and sit with Bonita," he said, his eyes shining with a brightness Bonita had to interpret as malicious, for he rarely spoke to Brad at all and, when he did, it was usually to say something curt or insulting. Bonita noticed Brad made no move to get up and relinquish his chair. Jordan came to stand behind him, and placed his hand on Brad's shoulder.

"I'm sorry I put the blame for what happened on your horse. I know you love that animal. I just spoke out in anger the other day and I apologize."

Both Brad and Bonita stared at Jordan as if he had spoken in some foreign tongue.

"I want you to know that no one in the company holds you or that horse responsible. It was just a freak accident."

Jordan's kind words seemed to be a sort of dismissal, giving Brad the cue line for a graceful exit, but he didn't take the hint and sat drinking his coffee, apparently trying to adjust to this new side of the man who had always before acted like an enemy.

"How are you feeling, Bonita?" Jordan asked, suspending his forced joviality to give her his usual brooding look.

She didn't know how to answer him. She wanted to blurt out that her emotions were ravaged with love for him, that she was so distracted with thoughts about him that she could hardly stay still in bed. Instead, she answered with ritual words that would reveal nothing.

"I'm fine, thank you." Then she couldn't help herself for inquiring, "Did I hear you having a talk with my grandmother?"

"Yes, we were discussing the script. You know, your grandmother is a very wise and discerning woman. She's given me all kinds of new insights into our scenario."

"That's nice," Bonita said, trying to hide the bitterness from her voice. He had never sought her suggestions on interpreting the script, and yet he was willing to discuss it at length with her grandmother and even acknowledge her help with it.

"She's made me understand all the characters a lot better. I think I'll approach some of the scenes differently." He was pacing up and down the small space beside Bonita's bed. "I'm glad we haven't filmed that scene yet where Doug finds Kate after she's run away from him. I have some new ideas on how to handle that and make Doug more sympathetic."

He seemed filled with the energetic enthusiasm that always took possession of him when he talked about his work, and she was sure that if Brad had not been there he would have gone on to analyze the scenes that were still left to be filmed. She knew she should be heartened by the fact that he'd come to see her, but since he seemed only interested in discussing his work, there didn't seem to be anything personal to his visit.

There was an empty pause in the room as they all came to the conclusion that three people, particularly these three people, make an awkward conversational grouping. Then a loud automobile horn outside sounded three times intrusively, and Bonita heard Marlene Webb's voice calling from outside.

"Mr. Producer, I'm waiting for you."

Jordan walked over to Bonita's window and looked down. "Marlene, is that you?"

"Yes, tomorrow's my big scene, you know. It's time for that special rehearsal you promised me."

Jordan turned to Bonita and said suggestively, "I have a *very* special rehearsal in mind tonight for that flirty frail."

Bonita closed her eyes as she felt the stab of his words. She couldn't bear to look at Jordan and know that he was on his way to a date with Marlene where he would surely direct her in a moving love scene, whether it was in the script or not.

Jordan leaned forward toward the window screen. "Wouldn't you like to come up and visit Bonita?" he called to Marlene. He was making a lackluster gesture to appear interested in the patient, Bonita thought.

"I'm sure Bonita needs her rest," Marlene's voice called back. "But I don't, so come on, Jordan, dear."

"Excuse me, I have something very important to take care of," Jordan said, and giving Bonita an odd kind of salute, his fingers almost touching his lips before they waved good-bye, he left the room.

"Thank goodness he's gone," Brad said. "Doesn't he love to put a person off guard? Imagine him apologizing to me."

"That was strange," Bonita agreed. "I guess he has to speak like an executive in charge of a studio and try to appear gracious sometimes."

"Well, now he's off to show Marlene a good time. I'll bet she's just loving all this."

"Yes," Bonita said. "She's a lucky girl. She's getting just what she wants out of life."

"And you are, too, aren't you, Bonita?"

"What I want right now is rest. Marlene was right about that."

"I'll do anything I have to do to see that you're happy, Bonita. I'm that fond of you."

"I know, Brad. You don't have to keep reassuring me."

"But you look awfully pale all of a sudden. Have I stayed too long? I don't want to tire you out. We have that date tomorrow morning, you know."

Brad stood up, and Bonita hoped he wouldn't come over and try to kiss her good-bye.

"Here, would you mind taking these cups downstairs with you?" Bonita was grateful to see her ploy work. Brad was too frustrated in gathering up the cups to think of anything else.

"See you tomorrow," he said. Then when he had left the room and Bonita was adjusting her pillows she looked up to see him peeking around the door jamb.

"By the way, in case you're worried about that horse of mine, he's just fine. Marti rode that Sugar Eater all over the hills today just to make sure."

Bonita smiled. She had worried about the horse, and she had asked her grandmother about it from her hospital bed, but Brad had noticed that she hadn't mentioned him tonight, and he must have felt she needed her mind put at ease before she would be able to rest comfortably.

"Tell him I forgive him," she said. "In case *he's* worried."

After Brad had gone downstairs Bonita got up and closed her bedroom door. She took off her robe, turned out the light, and then, before getting into bed, she stood in front of her window, placing her feet in a patch of moonlight that spotlighted the carpet. She felt confined in her room, as though on a stage too small to play out the drama of her feelings. She stretched her arms, trying to work out the stiffness that had accumulated from too much inactivity. Tomorrow she would have Brad drive her to some spot where she could see the ocean, where she could look toward a distant horizon and dream of going to new worlds and seeing new people. She had to put aside forever all her forlorn hopes of finding her true home in the arms of Jordan McCaslin.

She felt exhausted when she finally got into bed, as if the thought of a compromised future had taken all the vitality of life from her, and her sleep was troubled and unrefreshing.

The next morning Bonita came downstairs determined to cook her own breakfast and prove to herself that she was recovered. She looked all over the house for her grandmother, and when she got to the kitchen she finally saw her through the window over the sink, stooped outside between the rows of her vegetable garden wearing her wide-brimmed gardening hat.

How peaceful she looked, concentrating on her task. Bonita tried to draw courage from the sight of her invincible grandmother, a woman whose life had not been an easy one. She had been widowed as soon as she'd come to California, she had lost her only child when he was in the prime of his life, the beloved son who would have run this ranch for her. She had taken over the rearing of her grandchild when that child was in a devastated psychological state after losing her parents. She had been plagued with ill health and the problems of trying to manage her property alone.

And yet she hadn't let these major disasters kill her spirit. She had focused her attention on the small pleasures of life, her garden, her cooking, her Bible reading, her knitting, the land that surrounded her home. And she had pushed aside all her youthful dreams to concentrate on living day by day, giving all who knew her the impression of being completely happy with her life.

Bonita forgot all about breakfast and went out the back door. Her grandmother had just finished pulling the weeds from a row of newly planted seeds and was straightening up, one hand on the small of her back. Bonita rushed to put her arms around her.

"What a wonderful hug! You took me by surprise. I didn't hear you come outside."

"Bertie, I love you very much, do you know that?" Bonita said, kissing the baby-soft skin of her grandmother's cheek.

"I do know it, but I love you for saying it. No one should ever hold back the words of love, even when they interrupt an old lady at her gardening."

Alberta took off her big hat, and tossed it on top of her spade and trowel. Then she brushed the dirt from her hands and took Bonita's hand to lead her toward a bench under an arbor of climbing grapevines.

"Come and sit with me in the shade for a minute. I have something important to talk to you about."

"I hope you haven't been working too hard out here in the sun."

"I'm not the one to be fussed over. It's you that needs some worrying. You look so pale and unhappy this morning. Pinch your cheeks a bit and see if you can't bring the color back to them."

"Yes, Grandmother," Bonita said dutifully, smiling in spite of the heaviness inside her.

"Well, that didn't do much. Let's see if I can brighten up your face another way. You know I had a talk with Jordan last night."

"He said he enjoyed talking with you."

"I'm sure he did."

"I can't imagine he was very interested in hearing our family stories. Did you tell him about Mom and Dad?"

"Yes, not just about their accident, but the whole story, going right back to when they first met walking on the beach one day near Cypress Point and she found out he was her new neighbor."

"I'm sure he was his usual bored self."

"At first I thought he would be. After all, I said to myself, he already knows all about this. It's the story he's filming. But then I saw that he was just sitting there straight as an arrow, just sort of holding onto the arms of that old rocker and listening like it was a whole new tale."

"He claimed that his talk with you gave him a new perspective of the script."

"Indeed it did. You see, Jordan McCaslin has thought from the very beginning that the script is the story of your love affair with Brad Stark."

"What!"

"Bonita, you never once told him that it was your

parents' story. And since the boy and girl lived on ranches next door to each other, he just assumed you'd written about Brad."

"How could he have believed that?"

"Well, he said your story seemed so real he was sure it had to be based on first-hand experience. Then when he met Brad the description seemed to fit. Of course, Marlene didn't help any. That night he came here for dinner she told him it was common knowledge around here that you and Brad would be getting married sometime soon, and that she was sure you'd written your own love story."

"She said that?"

"That's what he told me," her grandmother answered.

"She knows that's not true!"

"Well, she must have had her reasons for saying it."

"She's the cause of this whole misunderstanding," Bonita said, close to tears.

She began to feel some dangerous new quakings within her. She'd never felt so betrayed by anyone in her life, and if Marlene had been in front of her at that moment, she would have unleashed an angry outburst at her. Marlene had decided Jordan was a valuable prize, and she had wanted him to herself with no competition. In her typically conniving way she had lied to him, making up an absurd story about Bonita being in love with someone, and using the love story as her proof.

"No, Bonita, I can't agree that she's to blame. It's your fault, too. You were so awed and intimidated by Jordan McCaslin that you didn't speak to him honestly. You were ashamed to tell him the basis of your story. If you had been completely open with him he would have known Marlene was wrong."

But Jordan had believed Marlene's fable. And every time he'd seen Bonita with Brad, the lie had been reinforced. No wonder he had held himself back from her, pushing her from him just when he seemed to want her. He thought she was committed to another man. Why hadn't she ever told him the truth?

"You're right, Grandmother. It is my fault. But can I ever make up for my mistake? Is it too late to set things straight?"

"There's no time to worry about that right now. I see Brad's truck coming up the drive."

## CHAPTER TEN

From the small arbor at the end of the vegetable garden Bonita had a clear view down the long dirt driveway that led to the ranch house. She clutched her grandmother's arm.

"Oh, no! Brad's coming to take me for a drive. I'd forgotten all about that."

"You just go along with him. He doesn't talk on and on like I do. You'll have lots of time to think about what I've told you," Alberta said.

Bonita accepted her grandmother's suggestion, and ran to the house to get her sweater. "Keep him busy. I'll be back in a minute," she called over her shoulder.

When she got into Brad's pickup she could see that he had a lot on his mind, too, and they rode silently together for a long time. Finally he asked, "Where do you want to go?"

"I'd love to take a walk at Point Lobos."

"That's fine with me," he said, and when they reached the end of the Carmel Valley Road at Highway 1, he headed southward toward Big Sur rather than turning right toward the village of Carmel and the Monterey Peninsula.

Point Lobos was a tiny jagged peninsula that echoed the massive beauty of the Monterey Peninsula and, unlike it, remained in a completely natural state, devoid of houses, golf courses, and hotels. The land had passed through the hands of many owners. Once in the free and easy days of the Mexican regime it had been won by a new owner in a card game. It had been the site of a whaling station, a shipping point for a coal mine, proposed as a town site, and grazed over by cattle. Finally it fell into the hands of an owner who appreciated the unique beauty of the place which had inspired one poet to call it "the greatest meeting of land and water in the world."

Now the 1200 acres were considered the crown jewel of the state park system, and the rangers had installed one unobtrusive roadway and numerous hiking trails so that anyone could come and explore the primitive beauty of its clifftop cypress trees draped with lace lichen, secluded coves, and the miles of rocky beach decorated with the cold wash of the Pacific Ocean surf.

Brad drove through the park entrance, stopping to pay the ranger at the gate the admission fee, and soon they passed through the dark forest of pines and were driving beside the water, with meadows of wild flowers on their inland side.

"Let's go all the way down to China Cove," Bonita suggested.

At the end of the road they parked the car and started up the trail across some rocks.

"I suppose it's too late to spot whales on their way to Mexico," Brad said, stopping to look out across the water. "Last time I was here you could see a water spout out there about every half minute."

"Oh, Brad. Look close to the rocks. There's an otter."

Bonita was cheered by the sight of her favorite animal of all the local wildlife. A gray California sea otter, just about the size of her dog Lark, was floating on his back in a bed of kelp, working away at a sea urchin or mussel he had balanced on his stomach. As soon as he'd finished it, he rolled over and disappeared down into the water to search out his second course.

Bonita turned to follow the narrow path. From its viewpoint above the water the trail turned landward, up across a knoll decorated with the varied shapes of cypress trees. Distorted by the forces of wind and weather, the still-living trees were green with foliage, the dead ones stark silhouettes against the sky, their bleached and twisted branches red with algae. Suddenly the trail took a sharp turn and, as always, the sight far below them took Bonita's breath away. They were looking down a steep cliff into the clear green water of China Cove. An old wooden stairway led all the way down to the sand and Bonita followed Brad, somehow making her way down the steps, too captivated with the beauty around her to watch where she was going.

They sat down on the sand and for a long time said very little. Brad sifted sand through his fingers, moving more nervously than Bonita had ever seen him. He made a couple of false starts, clearing his throat and attracting her attention, and then apparently changing his mind and showing her a sea bird or falling silent again. Bonita was finally pulled completely clear of her own musings by his distracted state of mind.

"What's wrong, Brad?" she asked. "You seem to have something on your mind."

"Well, I do, but it's kind of hard to put in words."

"You can say anything to me. We're good friends."

"That's just it, Bonita. Darn it, you keep acting like we're just good friends, or buddies, or something, and every time I try to talk about our future life together you change the subject, and here you're supposed to be so doggone in love with me."

Bonita's eyes widened with surprise. "I'm supposed to be what?"

"Well, all those movie people keep teasing me about how we're Romeo and Juliet or something. They talk about how you wrote this love story all about me. It's embarrassing. I don't know how I'm supposed to act. And you saw how Marti is afraid to come near me."

It had never occurred to her since her grandmother's startling revelation earlier that morning that there might be yet another victim in this sad misunderstanding. Of course, now all of Brad's strange behavior of late was explained. He had heard the rumors on the movie set and he had tried to act accordingly, gathering all his nerve to kiss her, and call her his girl, because he thought it was expected of him. A tremendous burden was suddenly lifted from her shoulders as she realized that Brad probably didn't love her at all. Their relationship had always been the simple one of comfortable friends until he heard the gossip Marlene had spread around about their great love and tried to live up to it.

Brad took one of her hands in his and looked at her with an apologetic expression. "I've always been fond of you, you know that. And I was flattered as all get out when I first heard about your being in love with me. I guess I just thought it made good sense for us to get together. But Bonita, you don't act like someone who's in love with me."

"That story I wrote was not about you and me. It was the story of my own mother and father. Remember, you bought your place from my Grandfather Beasley's estate. My mother used to live in your house, then my father came to California and lived on the property right next door. They met one day on a beach just like this one, and then they used to sneak back and forth to visit each other, or go horseback riding, but they didn't tell anyone they were in love. It was their secret until the day they married. After that, everyone knew they were in love. I'm sorry I didn't tell you a long time ago about my story, but I was too busy with other things to even notice what everyone was thinking."

"Then you're not in love with me?"

"No, I'm not in love with you, but I love you and I'll always want you for a friend. Now stop looking so relieved. You're supposed to be crushed to hear I don't love you." Bonita laughed, and Brad made an exaggerated attempt to turn his happy smile into a tragic clown's face.

After just a moment Bonita said, "I'm in love with Jordan McCaslin," and the words flew into the air like a flock of soaring gulls. She had spoken the words out loud for the first time to someone, and her love took on a thrilling aura of reality by the mere speaking. She jumped to her feet, startling some sandpipers that were poking about in the sand near the water's edge.

"I'm in love with Jordan McCaslin," she called to them as they hurried away. Brad jumped up and took her in his arms and the two of them jumped up and down together in the sand, Brad now caught up in her happiness.

"I'm in love with Jordan McCaslin," she sang.

"She's in love with Jordan McCaslin," he sang with her. But then he stopped her next jump, holding her earthbound, to say, "But have you told him that?"

"No."

"Well, then let's go, girl!"

They ran up the long flight of steps two steps at a time. When they paused to catch their breath at the top they noticed a group of tourists on the path who had been watching their antics on the beach. They laughed when they had breath enough, and hurried on to the truck.

"But where are we going?" Bonita asked.

"To find this snooty character you're so in love with!"

"But I don't know where he is."

"While I was waiting for you this morning, I saw one of the guys working in your barn, and he said they were all over at the Mission today."

"If that's where they're filming today, then that's where he'll be," she said, hoping her words were true.

As they drove toward the Carmel Mission, Bonita began to see the answers to many more of the questions that had plagued her recently. She had never understood why Jordan McCaslin was so hostile toward Brad, but now she knew that it was only because he was jealous of him. He had cared for her enough to resent the man he thought she was in love with. She remembered the way Jordan had criticized the male character in her story, telling Bonita that she cared about her hero too much to see his obvious faults. She had thought he was disparaging her own father, that somehow he had found out who the hero of her story was and was purposely trying to insult her. But she and her grandmother were the only ones who knew that, and they had never told anyone. So he was striking out at the character he thought was Brad, his rival. He had perhaps cast a rough-and-tumble actor like Doug Driver in the part just to try to show Bonita by contrast how weak and ineffectual he considered her love object.

Now that Bonita was observing the scenes through the proper lens, she could see them all in sharp focus. Jordan McCaslin had been acting like a man in love, there was no question about that now. The man who had sworn never to care for anyone again had fallen in love, and she'd been too blinded by her own growing love for him to even see it.

The small parking lot in front of the Mission was full of trucks and trailers, and Bonita could see through the wooden gates into the small church courtyard that the usually tranquil garden was swarming with people.

"I can't find a place to park, so I'm just going to leave you off," Brad said. "That way you can't change your mind."

"Don't you want to come with me and see if Marti Colton is here?" Bonita asked as she got out.

"What do you mean?"

"Maybe you don't even know it yet, but I think you're falling in love with that girl," Bonita said.

"I am?" Brad asked. "I mean, I haven't even had a chance to think about it."

"Well, now your mind is free to explore the possibility," she smiled at him.

"Quit stalling, Bonita, and get on in there and find Jordan," he said.

Noticing that she was still holding onto the door handle, he began to inch forward.

"Now you go and tell that man just what you told me and I think your future will be all taken care of," he said.

As soon as she had closed the door he drove away, smiling to himself with a far happier look than when he had tried to take charge of Bonita's future for himself.

Now faced with the moment she had long dreamed of, when she would tell the man she loved all the secrets of her caring, she considered what might happen. Suppose he admitted his love for her, but told her that a future together was impossible, that his bitter memories of the past were too great an obstacle for him?

Or perhaps he would tell her that he loved her a little, enough to be jealous of Brad, but that he didn't love her enough to commit himself to a lifetime with her. Would she be able to stand the pain of fresh disappointment? Her footsteps toward the Mission gates were not as eager as they had been on the beach, when she had first decided to go with all frankness and boldness to face up to this unpredictable man.

She was happy to see that everyone was occupied with setting up a scene near the door of the church beneath the Moorish bell tower. Jordan was too busy to notice her in the crowd.

The Basilica of Mission San Carlos Borromeo del Rio Carmelo, named in honor of a patron saint when it was founded two hundred years ago, had once been the pride of the founding father of the California missions, Father Junipero Serra. And it did not surprise Bonita to think that he had chosen it as his own home base from among all the missions he had established one day's march apart down the length of California. The setting, at the mouth of the Carmel River just where it meets the sea, with doorways looking up the low roll of hills into the green-purple haze of the verdant valley, was ideal. But after his death the missions were secularized, and the converted Indians who had made the place a vital community wandered away.

At the time of her story's setting at the turn of the century the Mission was in a frightful state of disrepair, a priceless relic neglected and awaiting restoration. The set decorators had recreated that time, placing broken-down carts here and there, making the adobe garden walls look as if they were crumbling, and adding weeds and boulders to the garden.

"Father, I must talk to you. I have to talk to someone," Doug Driver said.

He was rehearsing next to the stone facade of the church. An actor dressed as a priest came toward him, and Bonita stepped through a patch of blooming purple sage to get closer to the action.

Something had been changed. This scene was supposed to be played between Doug and the schoolmarm, but now Bonita could see Marlene standing with a sullen look on her face at the edge of the crowd. She was wearing another stylish outfit from the dress shop, and Bonita wondered why she wasn't in her costume and makeup.

Bonita saw Charlotte hurrying by with a stack of dresses over one arm.

"Isn't Marlene Webb supposed to be in this scene?" she asked her.

"Nobody ever tells me anything. Can you imagine, I got a call at midnight last night asking me to round up priests' robes in four different sizes? I guess Jordan was on the phone all night trying to find someone to replace Marlene."

"But why?"

"Like I say, no one ever tells me anything. The last I knew she was supposed to be in this scene. I spent all day yesterday trying to mend the pinholes in her costume where she'd been trying to change my fit."

"Quiet on the set, please. This is a rehearsal," the assistant director called out.

The scene worked beautifully. Bonita had to agree that the rewrite had been effective. Doug was properly anguished as he poured out his story to the priest, and the old priest was a compassionate listener. Bonita could see Marlene mouthing the words as the priest spoke, moving about the edge of the set like a stalking feline, obviously seething because her best scene was being played by someone else. But when Jordan bumped into her, backing away from the actors he was watching so intently, she responded in an unusually submissive way.

Jordan glared at her for a moment and then pointed toward the farthest edge of the garden. She accepted her banishment meekly, as if she knew she could no longer demand the limelight.

Bonita realized that Jordan must have confronted her last night with the lie she had told him. He had apparently decided he could no longer work with her in the picture, and he had replaced her with the hurriedly summoned actor who was now playing her big scene. Bonita felt that Marlene had been suitably punished for her duplicity. She was going to end up like the proverbial face on the cutting-room floor.

As Jordan watched to make sure Marlene went to the spot out of his way that he had indicated, he caught sight of Bonita standing amid the purple salvia blossoms. His look was too fleeting for Bonita to interpret, for at that moment Dan Evans came up to him and said, "The sun's moved behind the clouds again, let's get this next shot in the can as quickly as possible," and Jordan turned back to the business of picture-making.

The scene they were filming was supposed to take place at night, but Bonita remembered Jordan explaining to her grandmother that it was expensive to film at night under harsh spotlights that gave an unnatural brilliance. Instead, night scenes were almost always shot "day for night," meaning they were filmed during the day, but with a filter on the camera that darkened the setting. He had explained that the shadows from the bright sunlight then appeared to be caused by moonlight, but that most directors preferred to shoot such scenes on overcast days, for that created an even more convincing illusion of moonless nighttime.

The scene was perfect on the first take. The same sensitivity that Doug had shown in that brief monologue in the sneak preview in San Francisco was now expanded and explored. His tone of voice was restrained and pleading, and his usual wide gestures were held in check. She could almost imagine that her father would have said these words in the same way.

As soon as Dan Evans called, "Cut, print it," Doug jumped excitedly out of camera range, and now back in his own character he ran to pick up Kate Harrigan and whoop with his own pride at how he had played the scene.

Everyone else stood quietly awed by the scene that he had just played. It was always a source of surprise, even to these hardened professionals, when an actor was able to rise above himself and do his work in a new and more effective way.

During that brief hush of respect, Jordan McCaslin called across all the people between them. "Bonita, was that gentle enough for you?" There was no malice to his voice, only an unfamiliar appeal for her approval.

Kate Harrigan's eyes were shining with her enthusiasm, but her words were typically tart. "I thought the old cowboy was going to squeeze out a tear he got so carried away," she said, and everyone laughed to ease the emotion of the moment.

"I need a few minutes to consult with my author on some changes," Jordan called to his crew. "Let's take a ten-minute break."

Everyone hurried to his duties with a happy air of accomplishment. People bumped against Bonita as they moved equipment and props to the next position, but she stood stock still, watching Jordan walk toward her, ignoring all his associates who were vying for his attention. When he reached her side, he took her hand in his and began to lead her away with him.

"Let's get away from this madhouse," he said. "I think I know a spot where we can be alone. We have some major revisions to discuss."

"Revisions?" she asked, feeling a fearsome thud of disappointment.

"We're going to do a rewrite on our lives," he smiled.

She followed him through the great arched doorway into the church. It was dark and cool inside as they walked down the main aisle between the benches.

Beautiful plaster figures smiled lovingly at them from the altar, and she inhaled the heavy sweetness of flowers and candles in the air. Jordan led her out the side door of the church and down the long cloistered arcade that surrounded the inner quadrangle of the Mission.

They walked across the large empty space which had once been the hub of the Mission's activity for the one thousand Indians and padres who had lived there. Today it was deserted; there was only a breeze with them, filling the silent void with a soft rustling sound as it played among the relics of bygone days: an old grinding stone, a piece of harness chain, broken chunks of flagstone. Still holding hands, they came to the low wall surrounding the fishpond in the very center of the patio.

"I have to tell you the truth about my story," Bonita said.

"I know it now," he said. "Your grandmother told me last night. All along I thought we were filming the story of your great love for Brad Stark. I guess that's why I kept trying to turn the character into such a bad guy. I was jealous."

"You were jealous? Why, Jordan McCaslin. I was told you were impervious to such feelings."

"I was, Bonita. I wanted to go on making war movies and murder mysteries, and keep my heart out of the action. Until you and this fragile little story you wrote came along. The more I studied it, the more I knew that I loved you and that I wanted you to love me the way your character loved her man."

"I do."

"Then marry me, and let me give you the world."

Jordan stepped closer to Bonita and put his hands on her shoulders. "A great movie producer knows just how to stage an important scene like this," he said. "Now listen to me. Lift your head, look into my eyes.

That's it, smile adoringly. You take direction very well."

Bonita smiled up at him, confident at last that the exciting fantasies she had dared to dream were going to come true. He was offering her the world, and now with his love for her as a firm foundation, she could confidently step forward with him anywhere.

She was as happy for Jordan as she was for herself. Already the harsh planes of his face seemed softened, and the eyes that had always before shown the world a guarded cynicism were now cloudless, openly reflecting the blue of the sky with a look of trust in them that showed he knew he would never be hurt by the woman he was pledging himself to.

He laughed with the full enjoyment of loving her. "Now when I kiss you, close your eyes," he said, still the master of the situation.

Bonita didn't need a script. As soon as his lips touched hers she knew that she was in the right place, acting out the right scene. She had never felt so sure of herself.

Jordan stepped back for just a moment. "As far as I'm concerned only one man can play the leading role in your love story." And this time he kissed her without giving her any direction at all.

# Dell's Delightful
## Candlelight Romances

- [ ] **THE CAPTIVE BRIDE**
  by Lucy Phillips Stewart ............................ $1.50   (17768-5)
- [ ] **FORBIDDEN YEARNINGS**
  by Candice Arkham ................................... $1.25   (12736-X)
- [ ] **A HEART TOO PROUD**
  by Laura London ...................................... $1.50   (13498-6)
- [ ] **HOLD ME FOREVER** by Melissa Blakely  $1.25   (13488-9)
- [ ] **THE HUNGRY HEART** by Arlene Hale ..... $1.25   (13798-5)
- [ ] **LOVE IS THE ANSWER**
  by Louise Bergstrom ................................. $1.25   (12058-6)
- [ ] **LOVE'S SURPRISE** by Gail Everett ............... 95¢   (14928-2)
- [ ] **LOVE'S UNTOLD SECRET**
  by Betty Hale Hyatt .................................. $1.25   (14986-X)
- [ ] **NURSE IN RESIDENCE** by Arlene Hale ...... 95¢   (16620-9)
- [ ] **ONE LOVE FOREVER**
  by Meredith Babeaux Brucker ................... $1.25   (19302-8)
- [ ] **PRECIOUS MOMENTS**
  by Suzanne Roberts ................................. $1.25   (19621-3)
- [ ] **THE RAVEN SISTERS** by Dorothy Mack ..... $1.25   (17255-1)
- [ ] **THE SUBSTITUTE BRIDE**
  by Dorothy Mack ..................................... $1.25   (18375-8)
- [ ] **TENDER LONGINGS** by Barbara Lynn ..... $1.25   (14001-3)
- [ ] **UNEXPECTED HOLIDAY**
  by Libby Mansfield .................................. $1.50   (19208-0)
- [ ] **WHEN DREAMS COME TRUE**
  by Arlene Hale ............................................ 95¢   (19461-X)
- [ ] **WHEN SUMMER ENDS** by Gail Everett .... 95¢   (19646-9)

At your local bookstore or use this handy coupon for ordering:

**Dell** | **DELL BOOKS**
**P.O. BOX 1000, PINEBROOK, N.J. 07058**

Please send me the books I have checked above. I am enclosing $_____
(please add 35¢ per copy to cover postage and handling). Send check or money order—no cash or C.O.D.'s. Please allow up to 8 weeks for shipment.

Mr/Mrs/Miss_____

Address_____

City_____State/Zip_____

# Dell Bestsellers

- [ ] **THE MEMORY OF EVA RYKER**
  by Donald A. Stanwood ..................................$2.50 (15550-9)
- [ ] **BLIZZARD** by George Stone ..........................$2.25 (11080-7)
- [ ] **THE BLACK MARBLE**
  by Joseph Wambaugh ....................................$2.50 (10647-8)
- [ ] **MY MOTHER/MY SELF** by Nancy Friday ....$2.50 (15663-7)
- [ ] **SEASON OF PASSION** by Danielle Steel ....$2.50 (17703-0)
- [ ] **THE IMMIGRANTS** by Howard Fast .............$2.75 (14175-3)
- [ ] **THE ENDS OF POWER** by H.R. Haldeman
  with Joseph DiMona ......................................$2.75 (12239-2)
- [ ] **GOING AFTER CACCIATO** by Tim O'Brien ..$2.25 (12966-4)
- [ ] **SLAPSTICK** by Kurt Vonnegut .......................$2.25 (18009-0)
- [ ] **THE FAR SIDE OF DESTINY**
  by Dore Mullen .................................................$2.25 (12645-2)
- [ ] **LOOK AWAY, BEULAH LAND**
  by Lonnie Coleman ..........................................$2.50 (14642-9)
- [ ] **BED OF STRANGERS**
  by Lee Raintree and Anthony Wilson ..........$2.50 (10892-6)
- [ ] **ASYA** by Allison Baker ..................................$2.25 (10696-6)
- [ ] **BEGGARMAN, THIEF** by Irwin Shaw ...........$2.75 (10701-6)
- [ ] **STRANGERS** by Michael de Guzman ........$2.25 (17952-1)
- [ ] **THE BENEDICT ARNOLD CONNECTION**
  by Joseph DiMona ..........................................$2.25 (10935-3)
- [ ] **EARTH HAS BEEN FOUND** by D.F. Jones ....$2.25 (12217-1)
- [ ] **STORMY SURRENDER**
  by Janette Radcliffe ........................................$2.25 (16941-0)
- [ ] **THE ODDS** by Eddie Constantine ................$2.25 (16602-0)
- [ ] **PEARL** by Stirling Silliphant ..........................$2.50 (16987-9)

At your local bookstore or use this handy coupon for ordering:

---

**Dell** | **DELL BOOKS**
**P.O. BOX 1000, PINEBROOK, N.J. 07058**

Please send me the books I have checked above. I am enclosing $_____
(please add 35¢ per copy to cover postage and handling). Send check or money
order—no cash or C.O.D.'s. Please allow up to 8 weeks for shipment.

Mr/Mrs/Miss_____

Address_____

City_____ State/Zip_____

At last the sequel to *Beulah Land*
is now in paperback!

# LOOK AWAY, BEUL'AH LAND

### by Lonnie Coleman

For the plantation of Beulah Land and its masters, the Civil War ended in humiliation and destruction. Here are the characters you loved in the original story: Sarah Kendrick, the iron inspiration behind the struggle to rebuild the plantation; Benjamin Davis, determined to be his own man and strong enough to let no one stop him; Daniel Todd, a Union deserter; and Nancy, the freed slave whose toughness and gaiety lead her to a Savannah brothel.

Bound together by the affections of generations, Beulah Land's men and women set about creating a new way of life in *Look Away, Beulah Land*—a blend of past and future, perhaps stronger than the one they once knew.

### A Dell Book $2.50

At your local bookstore or use this handy coupon for ordering:

---

**Dell**  **DELL BOOKS**   Look Away, Beulah Land $2.50 (14642-9)
**P.O. BOX 1000, PINEBROOK, N.J. 07058**

Please send me the above title. I am enclosing $_____
(please add 35¢ per copy to cover postage and handling). Send check or money order—no cash or C.O.D.'s. Please allow up to 8 weeks for shipment.

Mr/Mrs/Miss_____

Address_____

City_____State/Zip_____